Harlequin Presents r ... ...e most gorgeous, brooding a... ...heroes—so don't miss out on this month's irresistible collection!

THE ROYAL HOUSE OF NIROLI series continues with Susan Stephens's *Expecting His Royal Baby.* The king has found provocative prince Nico Fierezza a suitable bride. But Carrie has been in love with Nico—her boss—for years, and after one night of passion is pregnant!

When handsome Peter Ramsey discovers Erin's having his baby in *The Billionaire's Captive Bride* by Emma Darcy, he offers her the only thing he can think of to guarantee his child's security—marriage! In *The Greek Tycoon's Unwilling Wife* by Kate Walker, Andreas has lost his memory, but what will happen when he recalls throwing Rebecca out of his house on their wedding day—for reasons only he knows? If you're feeling festive, you'll love *The Boss's Christmas Baby* by Trish Morey, where a boss discovers his convenient mistress is expecting his baby. In *The Spanish Duke's Virgin Bride* by Chantelle Shaw, ruthless Spanish billionaire Duke Javier Herrera sees in Grace an opportunity for revenge *and* a contract wife! In *The Italian's Pregnant Mistress* by Cathy Williams, millionaire Angelo Falcone has Francesca in his power and in his bed, and this time he won't let her go. In *Contracted: A Wife for the Bedroom* by Carol Marinelli, Lily knows Hunter's ring will only be on her finger for twelve months, but soon a year doesn't seem long enough! Finally, brand-new author Susanne James brings you *Jed Hunter's Reluctant Bride*, where Jed demands Cryssie marry him because it makes good business sense, but Cryssie's feelings run deeper.... Enjoy!

MISTRESS TO A MILLIONAIRE

*She's his in the bedroom,
but he can't buy her love…*

Showered with diamonds, draped in exquisite
lingerie, whisked around the world
in the lap of luxury…

The ultimate fantasy becomes a reality.

Live the dream with more
MISTRESS TO A MILLIONAIRE titles
by your favorite authors coming soon.

Available only from Harlequin Presents®.

Cathy Williams

THE ITALIAN'S PREGNANT MISTRESS

MISTRESS
TO A
MILLIONAIRE

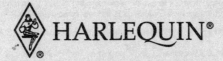

TORONTO • NEW YORK • LONDON
AMSTERDAM • PARIS • SYDNEY • HAMBURG
STOCKHOLM • ATHENS • TOKYO • MILAN • MADRID
PRAGUE • WARSAW • BUDAPEST • AUCKLAND

ISBN-13: 978-0-373-12680-4
ISBN-10:   0-373-12680-8

THE ITALIAN'S PREGNANT MISTRESS

First North American Publication 2007.

All about the author...
Cathy Williams

CATHY WILLIAMS was born in the West Indies
and has been writing Harlequin romances for over
fifteen years. She is a great believer in the power of
perseverance, as she had never written anything before,
and from the starting point of zero has now fulfilled
her ambition to pursue this most enjoyable of careers.
She would encourage any would-be writer to have faith
and go for it!

She loves the beautiful Warwickshire countryside
where she lives with her husband and her three
children, Charlotte, Olivia and Emma. When not
writing she is hard-pressed to find a moment's free
time in between the millions of household chores, not
to mention being a one-woman taxi service for her
daughters' never-ending social lives.

She derives inspiration from the hot, lazy, tropical island
of Trinidad (where she was born), from the peaceful
countryside of middle England and, of course, from her
many friends, who are a rich source of plots and are
particularly garrulous when it comes to describing her
heroes. It would seem from their complaints that tall,
dark and charismatic men are too few and far between!
Her hope is to continue writing romance fiction and
providing those eternal tales of love for which, she
feels, we all strive.

CHAPTER ONE

ANGELO FALCONE lay sprawled on the massive bed. Hectic, prolonged love-making had left the sheets half trailing to the floor and the rich burgundy damask quilt lay in inelegant disarray at the bottom of the bed. They had not bothered to shut the curtains and moonlight flooded the room, streaking across the heavy furniture in the room and lovingly illuminating the highly polished patina of wood.

He had properties in New York and Paris, but this apartment in Venice was by far his favourite. In every way it soothed his senses, with its unashamedly decadent opulence. It was the very opposite of the soulless minimalism that New York did so well.

And, of course, this was where he usually met her. Francesca Hayley.

Right now she was squinting down at the floor, trying to identify something she could put on amid the tangle of discarded linen and clothing that had been tossed in a pile in their mutual haste to touch one another.

He smiled at her thwarted efforts.

'You do this every time, Francesca,' he said with amusement in his voice.

'Do what?' She looked briefly at him and her whole body went hot under the lazy caress of his gaze. Crazy. She had met him thirteen months ago, had written him off as just the sort of wealthy playboy Italian she should steer clear of, and had continued to put up a determined fight until his charm, his wit, his perseverance had succeeded in crashing through her defences. It hadn't taken long. A little over a month.

'Insist on getting dressed as soon as you climb out of my bed. I like to see you naked. Why the need to cover up perfection?'

'I hate it when you say stuff like that, Angelo. I'm not perfect. No one is. Perfection doesn't exist.' She looked at him, stupidly shy in the face of his lingering appraisal. Perfection *did* exist. At least, physical perfection. Angelo Falcone embodied it. He was six foot two of dark, well honed, powerful male and what made him even more impressive was that his physical beauty was allied to a keen, restless intelligence. Together they formed a dangerously irresistible mix. She told herself this at regular intervals. It stopped her from harbouring unreasonable expectations.

'I beg to differ.' He folded his arms behind his head and continued to watch her. She was every red-blooded man's dream. A model without the shape of a stick insect and with a brain that often made him wonder what the hell she was doing in the superficial, fickle world of fashion.

'I still need to find some clothes.' She poked around the pile on the floor with one slender foot and gave up. 'I'm going to get something to eat. Do you want anything?'

'Come back to bed, Francesca.' He patted a spot next to him. 'You are quite capable of catering for my every appetite without getting me something from the kitchen to eat.'

Francesca grinned. 'Oh, dear. Is that the best cliché you can come up with?'

'Cliché? What cliché? I meant it.'

He was almost at her before she even realised that he was sprinting out of the bed, and she spun round and headed straight out of the door towards the kitchen, shrieking as she felt him closing the distance between them. No time to switch on any of the lights, but then no need either. Every curtain was pulled back, allowing the bright night sky to fill the open spaces of the rooms.

Angelo caught her from behind, but he didn't spin her around to face him. Instead he buried his head in her hair, breathing her in, wanting her more than he could remember ever wanting anyone in his life before.

Initially, he had decided that their frequent separations, when he was away on one side of the world and she was modelling on the other side, would be a good thing. Relationships, he had discovered, were prone to becoming stale. The first flush of lust very quickly gave way to the tedium of the predictable and there was no greater death to a relationship than predictability.

Not so with her. He missed her when she wasn't around. Lately he had found himself sitting in on meetings during which his mind had been at least half preoccupied with thoughts of when he would be seeing her again.

'We need to talk,' he murmured, wrapping his arms around her. 'I'm only going to be here for three nights, then I fly to New York for two days' worth of meetings, then on to London.'

Francesca felt the familiar flutter of disappointment, which she kept to herself.

'What are your movements? Any chance that one of your shoots might coincide so you could be with me in the States?' Did that have an air of pleading about it? He hoped not. Pleading was not his style. Nor, for that matter, was asking someone to accompany him on one of his business trips. Women had always been a background presence to his work life, but the thought of another week without her while he rushed all over the globe was not a thrilling prospect.

Francesca disentangled herself from him and switched on the kitchen light.

'No chance,' she said, with her back to him as she opened the fridge door and looked inside for something wholesome and quick. She had arrived at the apartment several hours before him and had had a chance to stock up on a bit of food. Still not looking at him, she now extracted some cheese and tomatoes.

'Right.'

'Not that I wouldn't love to, Angelo...' She was staring into the bread bin, which was bulging with some delicious Italian bread.

'Your work schedule is even more hectic than mine,' he said, keeping his voice light. 'I wish you would look at me when I'm talking to you.'

'I can't look at you and slice bread at the same time.' She paused and turned to face him, though. 'I really wish I could come with you, Angelo. I'd love to see New York with you, but you know you would be busy working anyway. We probably wouldn't have much time together. And you're right, my life is too hectic.' She shrugged and smiled ruefully. 'But then, I'm twenty-four. If I can't cope with hectic now, when can I? Not to mention the small fact that I have to earn a living.'

'Do you?' He paused, letting the significance of his question fill the silent space between them. Then he strolled over to where she was busying herself with the bread and cheese and turned her round to face him. 'You hardly lead a wildly extravagant lifestyle,' he murmured, cupping her face with both his hands and bending down so that he could deliver one of his wickedly seductive kisses. When he finally drew back, that brief spurt of anger he had felt at her refusal to accompany him on his trip was replaced by the satisfaction of knowing that this woman was utterly his. He touched her and she melted, and that was something he found intensely pleasing.

'I know you have your little apartment in Paris, but you rent that. So where does your vast fortune go?'

'Vast fortune is a bit of an overstatement.' The conversation was drifting into waters best left uncharted, and she eased herself out of his embrace. Tellingly, her body was still tingling in response to his kiss.

'Is it? I thought models only got out of bed if they were guaranteed shockingly large amounts for the effort...'

Francesca laughed.

She had a laugh that was infectious. It had been one of the first things Angelo had noticed about her. Standing in her little crowd of head turners, that rich, warm laughter had singled her out as the only one in touch with reality, with a sense of humour. And when she laughed she always tilted her head back slightly so that her long, straight dark hair rippled almost down to her waist. He caught her hair in his hands and curled his fingers through the silky mass.

'Are you telling me that I'm wrong?' he asked.

'I'm telling you that you're a dinosaur when it comes to snippets of information like that.'

'I'm thirty-four. A sensitive age. A man could be offended by a description like that...' He kissed the side of her neck, trailing his mouth along her shoulder blades while his free hand moved to caress one full breast.

Francesca could feel him hard against her and she moaned softly. When he lifted her fingers and began licking the taste of tomato and cheese from them, her moans became louder.

Not fair! How did he possess the ability to make her dissolve like this?

'You taste good.' He made appreciative noises that sent her senses reeling. 'Course, I can think of other places that would taste good as well, apart from your fingers. My appetite at this moment extends beyond bread, cheese and tomato…'

'Angelo!'

'Happy to oblige.' With that he ran his flattened palm over the firm lines of her belly, down to her thighs, nudging them open so that he could rub exploring fingers along her throbbing womanhood. Yes! Wet and waiting for him, and that felt so good.

He turned her to him and kissed her, a long, tender kiss that seemed to stretch into infinity.

After all these months their bodies had become attuned to each other but, for all that, there was no less of the shocking excitement whenever they touched.

He had never expected it to last as long as it had. She knew that, even though he had never said as much to her. He was a high-profile money earner who moved in high-profile circles and, as such, his reputation had preceded him.

He had moved through women like a connoisseur sampling fine wines, but only a glass at a time. A heartbreaker, one of her catwalk companions had confided. Francesca couldn't imagine ever having her heart broken, but she had still shied away from him, and even when they had become an item it had never crossed her mind that over a year later they would still be seeing one another.

She coiled her hands around his neck and returned the kiss with equal tenderness.

'Have I told you how sexy you are?'

'A number of times,' she whispered, dropping her head back, knowing that he would be unable to resist her breasts pushing against him.

Angelo propelled her towards the small, heavy kitchen table which was covered in a cloth of vibrant, swirling patterns and she lay back on to it, smiling drowsily with the anticipation of pleasure. She wondered whether whoever had fashioned this table would now approve of the unconventional use to which it was being put.

When he leaned over her and began tracing the outline of her nipple with his tongue, she had to fight the urge to maintain her control. They had already made love twice since he had entered the apartment a few hours ago, but she still wanted him now as intensely as she had when he had walked through that door into her arms.

She wanted him to smother her breasts with his mouth, and he did. And she wanted him to find other parts of her to explore, and he did, and she squirmed with pleasure when he did that.

It was still amazing for her to think that no man had ever done that act of intimacy with her before him, that her body had been embalmed in ice until he had come along and set it ablaze.

When he finally thrust into her she was on the edge of climaxing and they both came with a shudder that seemed to last for ever.

He was perspiring as he helped her sit up, just as she was.

'Better than a sandwich?' he teased, sweeping her hair away from her face and clasping it behind her neck.

'Much, much better than any sandwich and especially mine.' It was a running joke between them that her culinary skills were hopeless. He frequently told her that she would have to start learning how to cook pasta and her reply was always that a restaurant would do it better so why bother to try?

One day, she would solemnly promise, she would become a cordon bleu cook and then he would never be able to joke about her cooking skills again.

'But you're still hungry…hmm?'

'Fancy making me a sandwich?' she asked.

'What do I get in return?'

'What would you like?'

You in New York with me. You everywhere with me.

'We have something to eat and then I shall bathe you…'
As in every other area of his life, when Angelo prepared
something to eat he did it with style. The legacy of having
an Italian father, he told her as he grated mozzarella cheese
over the bread, added a touch of mustard and turned the
grill on. An Italian father, an Irish mother and a childhood
in downtown Chicago.

'I see the Italian,' Francesca mused, watching him as he
strolled naked through the kitchen, utterly at home with his
nudity. 'But where's the Irish?' He didn't often talk about
his past, only dropping the odd snippet here and there, and
she was hungry for more information.

'Would you have preferred me with red hair and freck-
les?' He handed her a plate and perched on the stool next
to her.

'It might have been very fetching.' She looked at his
raven-black hair, eyes almost as dark, and the harsh, an-
gular features that spoke of his Italian ancestry. The trea-
sured son. His parents had longed for a sprawling family
and instead had had to suffice with just the one child. Now
they were waiting for grandchildren. He had told her that
ages ago, when she had asked him why he was still a bach-
elor. He was going to live it up, he had told her, and then
settle down and, when he did, it would be for ever. He
didn't believe in divorce.

'And would you have fallen for that very fetching look?'
he asked softly, and Francesca hurriedly looked away.

Falling? No! They had never spoken about falling anywhere, had never once mentioned the word love.

'Red hair can be a bit tricky for a man to pull off,' she said, skirting around his question. 'You might have been bullied at school…' A less likely scenario she would have been hard pressed to imagine.

'You think so?' Angelo shot her a devilishly amused look from under his lashes. 'Can you imagine me being bullied?'

'No,' she said honestly. 'You're too scary.'

'You find me scary?'

'*I* don't, but I can see why some people might.'

'Why is that?' He caught the tail-end of her sandwich and took a bite from it.

'Don't tell me you don't intimidate people sometimes, Angelo. When you're doing one of these great deals of yours? When you're out to win something and someone's standing in your way?'

'I prefer to call it persuasion with intent.' He grinned at her. Extraordinary to imagine the freedoms she took with him. She had trampled all over his boundaries from the very start and she still did it, and he didn't care. That was the extraordinary thing. He had become cavalier with his cherished privacy and he didn't mind.

He thought about later, lying in bed, telling her what he had to tell her, picturing her face.

'Is that right?' Francesca said dryly. 'And I call eating this very fattening bread and cheese *flirting with a few calories*. When I put on vast amounts of weight and can no longer do my job, I shall blame you.' She stood up and headed towards the bathroom, chatting to him as she walked, knowing that he would be grinning as he looked at her from behind, appreciating every line of her body, which he refused to accept was anything but perfect.

In her quiet moments, she often thought of the price she had paid for her so-called perfection. Small lies she had told, cowardly lies that told him things she knew he wanted to hear, little images built up of her over time that bore no resemblance to the unsavoury truth. How had all those little lies become an avalanche? Francesca tried never to think about it. The temporary nature of their relationship made it easy.

'You'll have to give it up one day,' he said suddenly.

'Where did *that* come from?' Francesca turned to him, leaning lightly against the bathroom door, and raised her eyebrows in a question.

'A model's life is a short one by its very nature,' Angelo pointed out, pausing as he brushed past her to plant a quick kiss on her parted mouth. 'You know what they say about beauty. Here today, gone tomorrow.'

'You do know how to make a girl feel old.'

'And what will you do then?' He sat on the edge of the big free-standing bath with its clawed feet and switched on the taps, testing the water with his hands until the temperature was just right, before tipping in a liberal amount of bath foam.

The smile faded from her lips. For the first time since she had met him, he seemed different today. His mood was odd, swinging from teasing to gravity in the space of seconds, and it was disconcerting. Was she supposed to answer his question seriously? Or was she misreading him? Maybe he was tired. Exhaustion could do weird things and, face it, he had been on several long-haul flights over the past few weeks, barely leaving himself sufficient time to draw breath in between.

'Oh, I don't know,' she answered lightly, ignoring the shift in atmosphere. 'Maybe I'll start a new line of Francesca Hayley cosmetics. Isn't that what all ex-models do? Or I *could* go into acting...'

'Acting? I would never allow it.'

'I didn't realise that you would have a say.' She folded her arms and looked at him steadily, sure now that something was going on but uncertain as to what it could be.

'You're my woman. Of course I would have a say.'

'Whoa! All that arrogance! Your Italian ancestry is showing again.'

'You love it. Admit it.'

Love. There it went again. Francesca stepped into the bathroom and pretended to concentrate on the water, bending over to swirl her hand through it. 'Anyway, it's a crazy thought,' she said. 'I would never go into acting. I can't think of anything worse. All that falseness.' She shuddered and then it struck her that she was the last person who had any right to look down on people who spent their lives pretending. 'Tell me what you're working on in New York,' she said, changing the subject. 'Still that deal to buy property in Greenwich Village?'

'Wrapped that one up. I'm working on a joint venture with people in New York and London.' He switched off the taps and seemed to be lost in thought as he stared down at the water.

'Top secret deal?' Francesca teased, stepping into the bath and lying back with her eyes closed. 'Honestly, Angelo, I've told you before, only undercover secret agents have a right to be secretive about what they do.'

'You, my dearest, have no idea how the world of business operates. One wrong word in the wrong ear and bang, a deal can be flushed down the drain before you have time to draw breath.'

Francesca smiled, eyes still shut. 'You make it sound very exciting.'

'It is.'

'But you'll have to give it up some day, Angelo. You know what they say about stressful jobs and high blood pressure.' She opened her eyes and gazed at him with burning appreciation as he lowered himself into the bath opposite her. 'And you're not getting any younger. What will you do then? Perhaps you could consider a more restful career in your own line of cosmetics for men? The Angelo Falcone range of moisturisers?'

Angelo burst out laughing and, distracted for a few moments, he leaned towards her, ordering her to swivel around, which she did with some awkwardness, then he began to wash her hair. He did a very efficient scalp massage. She relaxed utterly, enjoying the feel of his fingers as he tipped shampoo into her hair and began working it up to a lather. It was way too late to be doing this, having her hair washed. She would never have the time to do a thorough job blow-drying it, but she didn't care. No work for the next few days. She could actually luxuriate in the blissful freedom of not caring how she looked.

'Hmm. That's a thought. Not sure I would be very good at it…'

'Why not?'

'Too much of a man,' he stated, using the attachment to begin rinsing the shampoo away.

'Oh, I see. Of course. Why didn't I think of that?'

'Don't know. You should have. It is not as if you don't know me. In fact, I would say that you know me better than any woman ever has before…'

'Is that a good thing, I wonder? Don't you think it's impossible to ever really know someone?'

For just a few heady, dangerous seconds she wondered how he would react if she told him how much he didn't know about her. The temptation didn't last long. Not when she conjured up the consequences. No more Angelo, and the thought of that sickened her even though she knew that there was no future between them. None at all. That was a bridge she wasn't going to cross just yet.

'Anyway, let's not be serious,' she coaxed, sliding back towards him and guiding his hands to her breasts. 'You promised me a lovely, pampering bath. You know we models have to be pampered.'

He pampered her. He doubted she could have enjoyed it as much as he did. He loved running his hands along her wet, slippery body, soaping every inch of her, taking his time. Then, when they were on the point of shrivelling from over-exposure to water, he towelled her dry very slowly and very carefully and absolutely forbade her to put on any pyjamas, even though over time he had chosen every single item of nightwear she owned. From the stunning model who was never seen in anything but the finest of designer clothes yet harboured an array of oversized tee shirts in which she slept, she had become the possessor of fabulously sexy nighties, flimsy things that barely skirted her beautifully proportioned body.

Tonight, though, he wanted to feel her nakedness next to him, wanted to be able to touch her at any time of the night without his fingers having to come into contact with material, however little of it there might have been.

'Are you happy, Francesca?' he asked in a low voice, when they were finally in bed and facing one another.

She looked at him, startled and unsettled by the question. 'What do you mean?'

'I mean,' Angelo said softly, stroking back her hair and running his thumb along the side of her face, 'we meet like ships in the night. I live out of a suitcase and so do you. It isn't satisfactory...'

'It's just the way it is. There's nothing we can do about it.' Her heart was beginning to beat faster. She could feel a fine film of perspiration break out as she frantically tried to think of ways to change the subject. Pointless. Angelo was persistent. She knew him well and she knew that he could be like a dog with a bone, the type of man who saw his goal in the distance and proceeded to get there whatever the obstacles presented on the way.

'Why do you say that?'

'You know why. Because my work involves a lot of travel. As does yours. Angelo. Do we have to talk about this right now? I'm exhausted. Honestly. It's late.'

'No time like the present.'

'Let's just leave things the way they are. You asked me whether I was happy and yes, I am. Very.' She smiled at him and closed her mind to the thought of what lay ahead. Over the past months she had become an expert at living in the present. It was such a good place to be.

'Happy seeing me now and again? Happy getting diaries out so that we can work out schedules and arrange our meetings like business partners trying to find a convenient date to see one another?'

'Whatever. Happy being with you when we do meet. It's good enough for me.' *Please, let's drop this.*

'There's no need for you to be based in Paris...'

'I have to be based *somewhere* and Paris is the most convenient place. I mean, my work is all in France or Italy, aside from shoots in the Far East.'

'Which is slightly odd, considering you are from England.'

Francesca went very still, but he didn't pursue that line of speculation. Instead he murmured gently, 'You must have some hankering to return to your roots. I know you've told me in the past that the only time to be adventurous is when you are young, but you could shift your base to London and continue to be adventurous.'

Francesca released her breath on a sigh. 'London,

Paris—where's the difference? You're still all over the place, Angelo, and I accept that. I'm not one of these women who wants to pin you down. You know you'd hate that, hate feeling as though you've been put in a trap—how many times have you told me that as soon as a woman starts smelling the aroma of permanence, you start getting restless?' She tried to lighten the atmosphere with a gentle smile. 'Maybe I prefer you to be with me now and again and wanting it rather than risk having you around more often, with the danger of you losing interest...'

'And maybe there is another option.' Angelo felt the sudden, overwhelming buzz of stepping off the side of a precipice. It was a more terrifying feeling than waiting on the edge of any big deal he had ever done in his life before. And to think that he had always considered himself a man who had gone beyond ever feeling that basic, gut-wrenching emotion called fear!

Francesca's eyes widened.

'I'm going to be setting up some pretty big ventures in London. Property. A couple of small architectural firms I want to get involved in. I've kept myself to America and Italy and now I intend to move to London, base myself there. Come with me.'

The world seemed suddenly to have tilted on its axis. Francesca sat up abruptly and drew her knees up, clasping her arms around them and leaning her head down in the posture of someone trying to fight off a sudden attack of violent nausea. She could feel the desperate thudding of her heart beneath her ribs, like a train that had shot its tracks and was gathering momentum in its free fall.

Eventually, she turned her head so that she was looking across at him.

'My work...' she ventured weakly.

'Could be done there. You no longer need to confine

yourself to catwalks in Italy. You can go into the magazine side of things. Don't tell me that's not a hell of a lot more lucrative. You can have lots more money to squirrel away.'

She heard the smile in his voice as he spoke and caressed her spine with one long finger.

'And there would be more time for us. Less travel for me… Who knows, you might find your homeland more tempting to your wandering soul if I were there, hmm? And things between us would no longer be this clandestine. We meet in this apartment in Venice or else in hotel rooms in various parts of Europe, and I weary of it after this length of time.'

'You're not meant to settle, Angelo. You said so! You have a wandering soul. Just like me.'

Angelo picked up the thread of panic in her voice and dismissed it. He was offering her something he had never offered any other woman in his life before, had never come close to offering! She was afraid that he would tire of her if they saw too much of one another, if they removed the breathless excitement of the clandestine. It was, he told himself, understandable.

'Are you not tired of wandering?' He frowned. 'Of intermittent meetings, making love knowing that time is not on our side because before too long one of us will have to leave to hop on a plane to somewhere? I want to be able to take you places with me, meet the people I work with, who work for me. I work in a very visible field. Expensive hotels and exclusive resorts. I want you on my arm, by my side…my perfect, well-bred, eminently presentable woman.'

Francesca felt sick. She couldn't remain crouched on the bed. She had to get up and move around. Without warning, she flung back the duvet and stuck her legs over the side of the bed, then walked over to the chest of drawers and yanked out some underwear and a tee shirt from the small collection of clothes she kept at the apartment. Yes, he was so right. Clothes that were a testimony to a life on the move. Some here, most in her flat in Paris, some already in a suitcase just in case she got a call and had no time to pack.

'What are you doing?'

Before she knew it he was out of the bed and coming towards her, and she hugged herself. Her legs felt cold but it was better standing up, made her stomach feel a little less queasy.

'It's not a good idea, Angelo.'

Panic, he could have dealt with. But the sudden flatness in her voice was like a punch in the gut. He gripped the sides of her arms with his hands and propelled her back against the wall.

'What are you saying?'

'Please, Angelo. Let's just leave things as they are. It works for us. Why fix it if it ain't broke?' She tried a laugh but it died as quickly as it had come, leaving the sour aroma of tension in its wake.

'You needn't be scared that spending more time with one another will jeopardise our relationship. We have been together for over a year. It is time for us to take the next step forward.' Angelo tried again but there was a beating in his head that was getting louder. Yes, he had been scared of jumping off the precipice into the unknown, but he had pretty much expected his landing to be soft. He certainly hadn't expected to find himself falling in thin air with the distinct suspicion that his landing was to be a bed of rocks.

'There *is* no step forward, Angelo.' She made herself do it. Made herself look at him straight in the face, and God, it was the most difficult thing she had ever had to do in her entire life. It made every painful turning in her life seem pale in comparison. And of course she knew why. Because she had fallen in love with him, hopelessly, blindingly and *stupidly* in love.

She watched the tenderness on his face replaced with disbelief and then his whole expression closed down and she didn't know what he was thinking any more.

'I don't want to play happy families with you. I was happy with things the way they were. It suited me.' She felt like a gravedigger digging her own grave.

'I see.'

No, you don't! You don't see anything at all!

'I don't want to return to England. Maybe one day, but not yet, and I don't want to move in with you and become your companion in this highly visible life of yours. If that's what you want then you're better off finding someone else to fill the role.' His eyes were hard and expressionless and Lord, it hurt.

'In that case there is nothing further to say.' He turned away from her and walked towards the door, only pausing when his hand was on the knob. Then he turned and gave her one final look.

'I am going to have a long shower. When I get out, I want to find you gone. Take all your possessions with you and, Francesca...' He allowed a few seconds of silence between them. 'Make very sure you never cross my path again.'

CHAPTER TWO

'IT's a short-list of three, Angelo, and really you *must* take an interest in this.'

Georgina wasn't happy. He could tell from the pursed set of her mouth and the way her slender, stiletto-shod foot was tapping impatiently on the floor. Angelo was very tempted to open a debate on the subject of exactly *why* he should take an interest. Hadn't he already taken enough of an interest to state what he wanted on the menu? He suppressed a little sigh of impatience and watched the down-bent head of his fiancée as she consulted a wad of papers on her lap.

Through the floor to ceiling windows of his impressive London office he could see the broad expanse of cloudless blue sky. English summers, he had discovered, lacked the vibrant heat of Italian summers or the stifling humidity of New York ones, but he rather liked their uncertainty. Cloudless blue skies one day, leaden grey ones the next. He shifted his chair back from his desk and went across to where Georgina was perched on the sofa.

'Let me have a look, then.' He took the sample menu sheets from her and sat down.

Animated at this show of interest, Georgina launched into a monologue on the various upsides and downsides of the menus. Which caterer presented what that would appeal to most.

'We have to get it *just right*,' she asserted. 'It's *our big day* and you know how many important people are going to be there. We just *can't afford* to have any slip ups.

Which is why I am recommending that we go with some-one we've heard of. Mummy's used the Walton brothers before and they're absolutely ideal. You just have to look at how they've presented their choices! Professionals.'

'Why are you asking my opinion if you have already made your mind up?' he queried. Of course he knew why. For, all her well-bred, sophisticated, self-assured elegance, Georgina tiptoed around him, never wanting to invite his displeasure. Which, he told himself, was as it should be.

'You're the one who insisted on authentic Italian food, darling!' She stroked the back of his neck lovingly and Angelo shook his head and stood up. He had decided. And it wasn't the Walton brothers with their impeccable pedi-gree. He was pretty sure that his choice would meet with a wall of resistance but that didn't bother him. Georgina would accept his decision without any show of temper.

'Who is Ellie Millband?'

'Darling, a friend of a friend of a friend used her to cater for one of their supper parties and apparently she's quite good, but probably not quite up to catering for the number of guests we have coming. Rather an amateur, I should imagine.'

'Her menu is interesting.'

'So are the others, Angelo.'

'And,' he said perversely, 'I like the thought of employ-ing an amateur. There is nothing more spiritually gratifying than knowing one is giving a helping hand to the under-dog.'

'Angelo, this is our *wedding banquet* we're talking about! Surely there is a time and a place for a social con-science!'

'Have you interviewed her?'

'I...I *honestly* didn't think that she would be a serious contender.'

Angelo tried hard not to frown at the creeping petulance in his fiancée's voice. *She's going to be my wife in exactly three months' time,* he told himself, and she was going to make him a perfect wife. Her background was impeccable, which was important for a man like him, a man who moved in the highest echelons. She was also devoted to him, reasonably intelligent and unquestionably beautiful. Five foot five inches of peaches and cream English beauty, with her china-doll blue eyes and her sleek, well-groomed blonde bob.

'Arrange an interview and I will see her. Will that satisfy you? You can trust me when I say that if she seems incapable of doing the job, then she will be dismissed from the running.' He strolled across to her and curved his hand behind her head, tilting her to face him. 'And we will go with your parents' recommendation. Hmm?' He smiled absent-mindedly at the beaming relief that greeted his suggestion, mind already ahead on the amount of work he had to get through before his dinner engagement later in the evening. 'But you'll have to leave now, *cara.*' He glanced at his watch ruefully and she sprang to her feet.

'I know, darling—work, work, work.' She pressed herself against him for a lingering embrace and pouted until he kissed her. 'Don't forget, Mummy's expecting us to dinner tomorrow evening so that we can discuss arrangements.'

'I don't think military engagements have been planned in more extensive detail,' he said, half amused, half irritated. 'And let me know when I can see this girl. If she's free later today I can squeeze her in around four-thirty, before I leave for the Savoy.'

'Oh, I'm sure she'll be available!' Georgina said airily. 'The prospect of a job of this size would probably make her willing to jump through hoops to please! But don't forget, *any sign* that she's not up to it and we don't give her the job. Promise?'

Her mouth was pouting for another kiss and Angelo obliged, hand on the door in the process.

'Absolutely,' he murmured. 'Now, òff you go, my sweet, and I shall see you tomorrow. I'll collect you at eight.'

'Seven at the latest, Angelo.'

'I'll do my best.'

She left a waft of expensive perfume in her wake and by the time the scent had faded he had totally forgotten about their conversation until he emerged from his two o'clock meeting to be informed by his secretary that Ellie Millband would be pleased to meet his future wife at four-thirty in the bar of a restaurant in Covent Garden.

'She's meeting me,' Angelo said, frowning.

'I believe she's only been contacted by Miss Thompson. Your fiancée rang to tell me that you will be conducting the interview in her place but she probably won't recognise you, Mr Falcone, as no doubt she's expecting Miss Thompson. Will that be a problem? I could always get in touch and—'

'No, no. No problem, Maisie. Just bring me in those reports on the Downy deal and buzz me at four or I shall forget and be in the doghouse with Georgina.'

Maisie, plump, fifty and the very soul of discretion, didn't so much as crack a smile at that fleeting conspiratorial tone in his voice, but, not for the first time, she wondered why he was marrying Georgina Thompson, who might carry the advantages of her well-connected family, but who lacked substance and who could be very cutting when her fiancé's back was turned and his ears were elsewhere. Not for a million pounds would she have shared those thoughts with anyone.

It was a little after four-thirty by the time Angelo negotiated his way to the American burger restaurant in Covent Garden which housed a long sports bar along one side.

It was, as he'd expected, packed. There weren't many nooks and crannies in Central London that weren't bursting at the seams with tourists in the middle of July and the heat seemed to have driven a fair few of them into the bar for something cold to drink.

Initial impressions were already beginning to leave a sour taste in his mouth. He hadn't wanted to concur with Georgina's prophecy that the woman was a rank amateur, but meeting in a busy burger bar in one of the most crowded parts of London to discuss what would be for her a very important job fell only just short of sheer stupidity. He imagined what Georgina's reaction would have been, had it been her standing in an uncomfortable queue by the door. She would have spun round on her very expensive heels and left without further ado.

If Ellie Millband's choice of venue was anything to go by then he was pretty sure that she had written herself out of the job but, having trekked across London to get to the place and with a bit of time to kill before he returned to his apartment to get ready for his dinner engagement later, he dutifully enquired of the small Australian girl clasping an armful of menus whether she could point him in the direction of a Ms Millband. He was startled to be told that she was downstairs in the restaurant.

'I'll make my way down myself,' he said, glancing at his watch.

'She's at the table to the back.'

Angelo nodded and headed towards the wooden stairs leading down, thankfully leaving behind most of the shopped-out hordes. It was cooler as he descended the stairs. It was also much emptier. In fact, so empty that only a handful of tables were occupied and, since three of them were filled with families, there left very little doubt as to whom he was going to see.

Yes, she was sitting right at the back, focusing intently on a small Filofax in front of her. Shoulder-length dark hair was tucked neatly behind her ears. Perfect ears. And, even though she wasn't looking at him, he would have known that face anywhere. He had seen it in his dreams for longer than he cared to remember and the mental image, even after three years, still had the capacity to fill him with burning rage.

Every muscle in his body kick-started into gear. He had to steady himself on the banister. Somewhere in his head, he knew that he should just turn around and go back the way he had come, then tell Georgina that *Ms Ellie Millband* was no longer a candidate for the job. His decision would have been final. He would not even have had to provide an explanation.

Common sense lasted the length of time it took him to blink, then he was walking towards her. In a moment she would look up and see him, see the man she had rejected three years ago. Anticipation of her shock made his pulses race with sadistic pleasure.

The wheel always turned full circle, didn't it? Not in a million years had he ever expected to see the woman again, but that hadn't stopped him from seeing her image in his head. He had striven to wipe her out and, to all intents and purposes, he had succeeded. His life had returned to its driving routine of work interrupted with the occasional fling until the passage of time had dictated that he needed to marry, to settle down and have the family he wanted. But her image had still persisted, creeping out to disturb the ruthless onward march of his career, always leaving behind the bitter taste of impotent fury.

He realised he was clenching his fists by the time he made it to the table. And still she hadn't looked up. Nor did he say a word. He just stood there until she was aware of a shadow looming over her. Only then did Francesca slowly raise her eyes.

The welcoming smile she had prepared for her prospective client faded into a strangled gasp. Nothing had prepared her for this. What was Angelo Falcone doing here? Was he really here? Standing in front of her? She blinked a few times, willing the image away, but he was still there, bigger, leaner and a whole lot more forbidding than she remembered.

'Surprised to see me, Francesca? Sorry, it's now Ellie Millband, I believe?'

'What are you doing here?' Francesca whispered, fascinated by the familiarity of his face and terrified at the harshness stamped on it that she had never seen all those years ago when she had been going out with him.

'Interviewing you, in point of fact.' He nodded at a passing waitress to come and take his order for a drink, then he sat down and gave her the full benefit of one long, insolent, unapologetically cold stare. 'Although whom exactly am I interviewing?' he asked silkily. 'Since you seem to have changed identities.' His initial shock at seeing her had given way to ice-cold self-control.

Francesca's brain cranked into gear. 'I was expecting to see…'

'My fiancée.'

'Your fiancée.' In her head, he had remained a single man. Stupid, considering the amount of women who would have swarmed around him, hoping to net the biggest fish in the sea. She stared down at her Filofax in confusion, then reluctantly looked at him. Her hands were trembling and she clasped them tightly together on her lap, well out of sight of his black, impenetrable stare. 'Congratulations,' she said belatedly. 'I…that would be…to Georgi…'

'So *who are you*?' Angelo interrupted. 'Shall I call you

by your new name, or was your old one the fabrication? Tell me. I'm interested.' Her hair was shorter but she looked even better for it and, even though the clothes were different, a tailored suit as befitting someone being interviewed for a big job, he could see that the body was still the same. Still that superbly proportioned body that had once driven him wild.

The memory of how she used to affect him didn't soften him. It was laced with too much bitterness.

'Francesca Hayley was the name I used when I modelled,' she said, steadying herself by breathing in deeply. 'I no longer model. Look, Angelo, I'm sorry to have wasted your time, and your fiancée's, but I don't think there's any point in our having this conversation.' She half rose, fumbling to reach for her handbag, which was on the floor by her chair.

'Sit back down, Francesca.'

His voice was calm and modulated but imbued with threat. Francesca hastily sat back down. *I'm Ellie Millband*, she wanted to tell him, *Ellie Millband, not Francesca Hayley*, but the words wouldn't come out and, anyway, he wasn't going to be prepared to let the past rest.

'We're old friends and ex-lovers…' His smile sent a chill of fear racing along her spine. 'Surely it would be fitting that we fill in the gaps in our respective lives now that fate has brought us back together?'

'There's no point, Angelo.' She had to steel herself to look at him. She recognised the lines of his face, the masculine beauty that she had once found so compelling, but she still felt as though she was sitting opposite a stranger and a stranger who could barely conceal his dislike. 'I came here to discuss, well, my ideas for a meal…for your wedding. I didn't come here to discuss the past.'

'Which just goes to show that we should always be flexible, don't you think?' His drink had arrived, something strong in a short, squat glass, and he accepted it without taking his eyes off her face.

With a painful stab, she realised that he was enjoying himself, enjoying this unexpected encounter. His life had moved on and he was more than happy to watch her squirm in front of him. She really couldn't blame him. If her legs would only start functioning properly she would have denied him the satisfaction, but she had a sneaking suspicion that they might just pack up from under her if she tried to stand up. The sensible mineral water she had ordered twenty minutes before when she had arrived, eager and early, now seemed ridiculously lacking in any ability to fortify her.

'What do you want to know?' she asked tightly.

'Tut, tut. Anyone would think from your tone of voice that you weren't pleased to see me. Strange, considering you were the one who ended our relationship.' The old, familiar rage formed a knot in his stomach. 'Let me see. What do I want to know?' He took a sip from his glass and stared at her over the rim, his sharp eyes taking in the jerkiness of her hand when she reached for the glass of water. Revenge was an unworthy emotion. He knew that, or at least the cool, logical, intelligent side of him knew it. Right now, though, he could taste the sweetness of it on his tongue and was inordinately pleased that he had not walked away when he had spotted her sitting at the back of the room.

'I am surprised you gave up your very lucrative modelling career,' he mused. 'What went wrong? Europe too small to contain the both of us?'

'It seemed a good time to come back to England.' Francesca raised her chin stubbornly, refusing to let him push her into a corner. 'I'd saved enough money to buy a small place of my own and I fancied a change of job.' Their eyes tangled and she felt hot and faint and agonisingly aware of the powerful effect he still had on her. 'It's no bigger a life change than the one you've made,' she continued. 'You've moved to London and become engaged. I'm sorry I didn't get to meet her and I don't suppose I will now, but good luck for the future.' Her mouth smiled politely but her eyes remained misty with a frantic desire to get away from his presence.

'And you? Not involved with anyone?'

Francesca thought of Jack, who would be wondering how the meeting was coming along, and her momentary hesitation answered his question. It was an answer he didn't care for and Angelo felt base, primitive jealousy rip through him like a knife.

'But of course, you would be,' he said smoothly. 'A beautiful woman like yourself.'

'There's no need to compliment me, Angelo,' she said sharply. 'You hate me. Which is why I can't understand what we're doing here, pretending to make small talk.'

'Hate? There is no mileage in hate. It's a counter-productive emotion.' He realised that his glass was empty and resisted the temptation to order another drink. Apart from the stupidity of drinking at this early hour, there was also the small technicality of a certain high-level dinner engagement later that evening. Which he was in danger of reaching late if he didn't make a move soon. He settled back into his chair and beckoned the waitress across. To hell with it. Another whisky and soda would be okay but he better make it a light one.

'So indulge my curiosity and tell me about him. After all, you know all about my personal status.'

'There's no one.' Poor Jack. She was pretty sure he wouldn't like being labelled as *no one*, not least because she had known him since her early teens, but she didn't want to start walking down the road of little lies. Although, did it matter any more? Once she left this place she would never see Angelo Falcone again. She certainly wouldn't be getting the plum job for which she had come so prepared. The wad of recipes she had painstakingly selected to bring with her were still sitting in her capacious bag, making a mockery of her high hopes.

'Ah, Francesca.' He raised his glass to his mouth and sipped carefully. 'You may have lied to me about your name—'

'I didn't lie to you! Millband is my mother's name and Ellie was always my first name. I didn't conjure the name Francesca Hayley out of thin air!' One little truth.

'But you're lying now. Who is he? Do you think I care?'

Of course he didn't care! Nor did she. On that very last evening he had told her that they were ships that crossed in the night. Now they were ships sailing different oceans. They no longer had any impact on one another.

'His name is Jack,' she offered with a little shrug. 'He works with me. We set up the catering business together, if you must know.' She stared down into the unappealing glass of water and then reluctantly took a small sip. It had been cold forty minutes ago. Now it was metallic and tepid.

'Jack. And how did you meet him? An ex-model also seeking to expand his horizons?'

For the first time since she had sat down, Francesca smiled with genuine amusement. Jack might have once upon a time been the sought-after boy in town, in the way that bad boys often were to teenage girls, but an *ex-model*? She thought of his shaved head and the embarrassing tattoos on his back and grinned. She couldn't help it. Then she laughed. That warm, rich, full-bodied laugh that was so infectious.

'I think he would be insulted if you called him that!

Well, that would be after I'd picked him up from the ground in shock at the description!'

It was that laugh that did it. Took him back through the years, took him back to that place where he had been captive to her irreverent ebullience. *She* had certainly never tiptoed around him. More ran circles around him

'No ex-model?' Angelo smiled at her with cold indifference. 'What, then? A businessman? Someone in a two-piece suit and a bowler hat?'

'Your Italian ancestry's showing, Angelo. Men these days don't wear bowler hats.' And people shouldn't find their past creeping up on them stealthily like a thief in the night. 'I really think it's time I left,' she said quietly. 'I'm sorry. This has been a shock…'

'But what about your menus?' Angelo asked. 'I wouldn't want you to return to your little house without at least giving you the benefit of telling me what you had in mind for my wedding banquet…'

'Stop it!' Two bright patches of colour had appeared on her cheeks. 'I always knew you were hard nosed, Angelo. I never realised you were just downright cruel!'

'Cruel? How am I being cruel? Explain to me. I meet you here after three years and am polite enough to ask you what you have been up to in that time. I offer to see your menus, which I assume you have brought with you. Hardly the definition of cruelty.'

'You know what I mean.'

'I have no idea what you are talking about. Time has a habit of dimming our memory of past acquaintances and their expectations.'

There wasn't a flicker of warmth on his face. He had found himself in her company before he had had time to retreat unnoticed and had managed to dredge up some semblance of politeness because the situation demanded it. A show of interest in her menu cards was just extending the politeness to embarrassing levels as far as she was concerned. The anger and dislike was there, she could feel it simmering behind the mask, but it was anger that had been roused by seeing her out of the blue. She doubted that he had given her much of a passing thought over the years or, if he had, only insofar as she had damaged his ego. Now, to him, she truly was an ex-acquaintance with whom he had shared a few months of his life, off and on.

He was engaged to be married. He had found love and affection and was eagerly planning his wedding day. She took a deep breath and tried to control the emotions beating against their constraints.

'You're right.' She ventured a smile which didn't garner a response. 'Okay. You can have a look at the menu I've prepared.' She rummaged around in her bag, feeling his eyes on her, and extracted neatly collated, printed sheets of paper. A choice, she told him, focusing on the papers and not on his face. Several options for starters, main courses and of course there would be a selection of desserts. She had only a vague idea of numbers but assumed that there would be roughly two hundred people from what his fiancée had communicated to her on her answer machine. Was she right in that assumption?

It was bizarre, sitting here like this, pretending to talk about a job that would not materialise while her heart did crazy things inside her and her head reeled with a sickening slide show of images of the past. She must have stored up so much information and, like a computer, her mind was now downloading it all in every painful detail.

What a joke to be sticking a phoney smile on her face and pretending that they were just two people having a normal conversation about a normal topic.

'What is she like?' It was spoken before she had time to think.

'I beg your pardon?' Angelo looked up at her politely.

'I'm sorry. I meant…well, I'm glad you've found someone you love, someone to settle down with. I'm really happy for you, Angelo…'

And she had found someone as well. Time had moved on. But he certainly wasn't happy for her, nor was he in control of his response. He inclined his head curtly in acknowledgment of what she had said and then returned to the menus. She had never been able to cook when he had known her. An omelette had presented a challenge. Now the array of food she had listed was exquisite.

'I wanted to do something that had a career in it but wasn't office-based,' she said, tuning in to his thought patterns. 'Hence the catering.' The fact that she had left school at sixteen without any qualifications to speak of had also dictated a life-plan that didn't include a university degree. That, she kept to herself. 'Once I had bought my house and was grounded, I found that I actually had to prepare meals for myself and I discovered that I enjoyed it. It seemed natural to take it one step further.' And specialising in Italian food had seemed natural as well, all wrapped up as it had been in memories of him. It had been a wise choice, as it turned out, for more practical reasons, because not many caterers specialised and very few specialised in Italian cuisine. She had found a ready market among the many well-to-do Londoners who held dinner parties and office dos and either couldn't be bothered or preferred to have someone else do the catering for them.

'How very resourceful. And how very puzzling that you were so eager to settle down. When we last spoke you were fighting the idea.' Or maybe, he thought icily, just fighting the idea of doing it with him.

'I know. I still thought that I wanted the adventure of never being in one place for too long, but…well…'

He watched the faint embarrassed blush creep into her cheeks, the way she tried to conceal her expression by looking down. He saw the truth staring him in the face. She had settled down because she had found the right man and it hadn't been him. It had never been him and, who knew, maybe this other man had been on the scene all along? After all, it hadn't been as if he had kept tabs on her. They had spent many periods of time apart, pursuing their separate careers. There would have been ample opportunity for her to have had someone else in the background. Someone else making love to her, turning her on. It was a thought that had not crossed his mind before but, now that it had, it took root and rapidly sprouted poisonous tendrils that curled into every corner of his mind.

'For the best,' he said into the tense silence. 'As most things turn out to be, in my opinion. After all, have we not both found our perfect partners?' His head seethed with images of her betrayal. Three years and he was discovering that the rage he felt towards her had only been papered over.

Francesca looked at him uncertainly, wondering what was going on behind the polite words.

'I have come to a decision,' he said abruptly, handing her back her papers and pointedly looking at his watch. A man on the move. A busy man who had only so much time to spend walking down a mildly interesting memory lane. He stood up and left sufficient money on the table to more than cover the cost of the drinks, ignoring her protests as she stuffed the papers back into her bag. He likewise ignored the businesslike outstretched hand as she half rose to her feet.

'That's okay,' she said quickly. 'I understand. Neither of us expected… Good luck with your wedding.'

'You have the job.'

It took a few seconds for what he'd said to sink in, during which time Francesca stared at him in blank amazement. 'What?' she stammered.

'You heard me. You have the job. You'll be hearing from me within the next week.'

'But I don't want the job!'

Angelo paused to focus all his attention on her. 'Reason being?' he asked softly.

'Reason being that we used to be lovers, Angelo! We can be adult and have a conversation because we have no choice, but there's no way that I'm prepared to work for you! It would be...*a joke*! And how do you imagine your wife-to-be would feel knowing that the woman providing the food for her wedding is her husband's ex-lover?'

'I am glad you used the term *ex*. And why on earth should Georgina be aware of the fact that once, years ago, we had a fling? It is an irrelevance. I am hiring you on the basis of the fact that I like your menu.' He didn't bother to pretend to himself that this excuse was even close to the truth. He had only to choose a caterer, order them to do precisely what he wanted, and they would oblige. Money always made people very amenable, and money was something he had in bucket loads. No, he wanted to cure himself of the gaping wound caused by her treachery. He wanted to still his raging mind from the torturous knowledge that he had been used like a plaything while she cavorted with another man behind his back. He wanted her in a position from which he could exact long overdue revenge.

'I don't want the job. Thanks all the same.'

'I don't believe I offered you a choice.'

Their eyes clashed and Francesca refused to look away. 'And what influence do you have over what I decide to do, Angelo? Are you going to throw me into a dungeon somewhere if I don't do what you want?' She gave a short laugh of disbelief. 'We're not living in the Middle Ages and you're not my master! I can get by without this job just nicely!'

'Can you, though?' He made a show of mulling it over. 'Really, I have found that London is a very small place. One word in the right ear and...' He gave an exaggerated helpless shrug that left her in no doubt as to the implication of his threat. 'I mean, how would it seem to prospective clients were they to know that you had turned down the job of a lifetime because you were afraid that you would not be up to the task?'

'You wouldn't.' But the colour had left her face. He would. He would destroy what she had built up because once upon a time she had bruised his manly ego. It was an insane reaction, but she knew that underneath that highly sophisticated exterior he was all Italian. It was what made him so potently attractive—the passion behind the steely self-control. She felt faint.

'I might not,' he conceded magnanimously. 'But are you willing to take the chance? To lose what you have? Your boyfriend works with you, which I assume means that you may well be jeopardising his future as well as your own—'

'Why? Just to even old scores? Is that it, Angelo?'

'A concept as old as the Bible,' he mused. 'But I also like what you have to offer. Why do you think I chose to interview you in the first place? Georgina said that you were a horse with little more than an outside chance. You should be flattered. Now, I really should be going. I have a business engagement later and I expect you will want to hurry home to that cosy little house of yours and start talking over preparations with your...partner, hmm?'

'Angelo...'

'You're not *scared*, are you, Francesca? Because you'll be in contact with me?'

'No, of course not!'

'Good. In that case, I will be in touch. I have your number.' He smiled but his eyes remained coolly dismissive. 'See this job as a challenge, your big opportunity to work on a slightly larger scale than you have been accustomed to in the past...'

'Too large a scale!' she inserted quickly.

'You should have thought about that before you sent in your tender.'

'I wouldn't want to let you and your fiancée down.'

'Believe me, I'll make sure you don't.' He left her without looking back and she remained standing at the table, barely aware of the waitress coming over with the bill, taking the money and returning with change. After the initial shock of seeing him, she realised that her body had gone into automatic mode, dealing with his questions, behaving as though she wasn't on the verge of hysteria.

Now that he had gone she felt as though she had been put through a wringer. She knew that she had never managed to exorcise his memory, but she had not been prepared for just how much he still affected her. Every part of her body was stretched to breaking-point and there would be more to come. More contact with him. More painful reminders of what she had been obliged to leave behind. There was nothing she could do about it. She didn't need the job but she couldn't afford to lose clients. He had caught her neatly in a trap and all she could do was get through it without too much damage being inflicted on her in the process.

CHAPTER THREE

ANGELO timed his call perfectly, as he timed all things. He waited just long enough for her to stew but not so long that she had time to think up any flimsy excuses to back out, because now that he had seen her he knew that, in the deepest recesses of his mind, she had remained unfinished business.

He pushed himself back from his desk and inclined his chair so that he could stretch out his long legs in front of him. The past couple of days had involved a delicate balancing act with Georgina who, after her initial dismay that he had decided to go with an unknown act, had been ready to move into action and take over the arrangements with her mother. Informing her that he would be personally involved in the process, he had met with a brick wall of understandable incomprehension.

'It's not necessary,' Georgina had complained. 'Mummy and I—'

'—will, I hope, respect my wishes?'

'But I don't understand—'

'What is there not to understand? You wanted my involvement and now you have it.' Put like that, it was left to Georgina to try and quantify the level of involvement she had been expecting but, while he had listened with every show of appreciating what she was saying, he refused to budge and in the end she had been obliged to accept that he would more or less be running the show.

He reached for his mobile and rang the number on the

business card that had been burning a hole in his wallet for the past three days.

Francesca answered almost immediately and, for a split second, hearing her voice down the end of the line was a brutal reminder of how they once used to talk on the phone, sometimes for hours on end, long, lazy conversations that made the physical distances between them seem less impossibly far.

'It's Angelo,' he said abruptly.

'How are you?'

'Is your diary at hand? We can arrange a time to meet so that we can discuss these menus in detail.'

'Angelo… I'm really not sure whether I'm equipped to cater for such a large number of people…'

'Haven't we covered that particular patch of ground already?'

'But—'

'I can meet with you and your partner tomorrow evening. Georgina will naturally want to come along as well.' Long, sexy conversations three years ago, when talking to her had been like a physical release for him after a gruelling day at work. He could remember her soft voice catching on a laugh, the way she had lowered it whenever she'd told him how much she was missing him, missing making love to him. He wondered now whether she had been saying the same things to someone else, someone more indispensable to her than he had ever been. 'Six-thirty at the bar in the Savoy,' he told her curtly. 'I'll expect you both there.'

Francesca was treated to the click of someone ending a phone call before she had a chance to speak and, with a little sigh of resignation, she turned to Jack, who had been sitting at the kitchen table, listening in on the phone call.

'It won't be as bad as you think,' was the first thing he said when he saw her face.

Francesca looked at him and smiled reluctantly. Jack knew enough about the situation to appreciate the awkwardness of it, but he knew nothing of the depth of feeling she had carried around with her for years, the knowledge of love lost for reasons beyond her control.

'No, it'll be worse. I wouldn't be surprised if he gets us there so that he can shake his head at what we suggest and conclude that we're not up to scratch for the job.'

'That would make him a very bitter man.'

'You've got it.' And it was a situation that never should have arisen. She should never have met him, should never have fallen in love with him. Theoretically, she should have fallen in love with the man sitting opposite her at the table. Same age, same background, same friends, most of whom they had long left behind, but still...

The beauty queen of the local comprehensive school with the highest truancy rate in the country should have ended up with the wild, reckless but irresistibly handsome badboy heartthrob, but fate had had other plans in store. Fate had decided to throw friendship into the cauldron, and friends they had become to the exclusion of everything else.

'Must have been a shock, seeing you,' Jack said with a wicked grin. 'Maybe he's still got the hots for you.'

'Oh, please. That was years ago. No, what he wants is to see me fail because I had the temerity to turn him down years ago and Angelo is not the sort of man who takes kindly to being turned down by a woman.'

'We won't fail, Ellie.'

'He calls me Francesca. For him, I'm the one who strung him along, rejected him only to run off and begin a new life with you.'

'Which is kind of true, in a way.'

'But not in the way he thinks. He thinks that we're an item.'

'And maybe it's safer that way,' Jack said thoughtfully. He leaned forward and rested both elbows on the table. 'I mean, he won't try anything if he thinks that I'm on the scene, will he?'

'Try anything like what?'

'Bit of a kiss and a cuddle in the larder?'

'The man's engaged!'

Jack shrugged. 'Fat lot of difference that would make to most men.'

'Jack, you're…you're…'

'Totally realistic?' He grinned affectionately at her. 'Think that's why I don't have any success with the ladies?'

'You have lots of success with the ladies, Jack McGill. You just don't want to take the plunge.'

'Because I'm realistic. I know the minute I step off the diving board I'm going to be thinking about swimming to the side of the pool and hopping on another one.'

'I give up on you.' But she never had and she knew she never would. They were tied to one another with bonds too strong to break.

'But the man obviously still has some effect on you.'

'Because I know him! I know he could destroy our careers for no better reason than getting revenge!'

Jack ignored the interruption. 'And it might be a good thing, in a way, that he's come back into your life. Maybe seeing him at close quarters, seeing him with his woman, you'll be able to put the whole thing into perspective and get on with your life. You'll be able to get him out of your system once and for all. You can't end up an old maid, Els. Fate worse than death when there are so many eager chaps out there waiting to snap up a beauty like you.'

'Oh, silly, selfish me, not looking at it from that point

of view,' Francesca said dryly, but maybe, just maybe, he had a point. Maybe she *needed* to see Angelo Falcone, needed to see him in the company of his fiancée, embarking on the greatest adventure of his life, before she could fully move on from the past. Like it or not, the past had held her captive for too long.

'Knew you'd agree with old Jack. And we could pretend to be an item if it makes it easier. A fair few women have told me what a sexy hunk I am.' He folded his hands behind his head and looked smug. 'Which just goes to show that bald men can still pull the birds.'

Francesca didn't think for a minute that Angelo harboured any feelings towards her, bar the obvious one of wanting to see her suffer, but it certainly felt more reassuring thinking that Jack was some sort of emotional barrier between them.

Lord only knew how he intended to play the role, but she had given him sufficient warnings about what he was to say and what he wasn't. The upshot was that he had agreed to talk only about the food, with which he was inordinately talented. In the event of any pregnant pauses, she'd informed him, he was to rush in with illuminating chat on regional Italian cuisine, which was something he knew more about than most Italians, especially considering he had never set foot on Italian soil. Under no circumstances, she'd warned him repeatedly, was he to indulge in any chit-chat about the past.

'Talk about the food, sit and look pretty.'

'Pretty might be pushing it,' Francesca had countered but, the following day, she had to admit that he had scrubbed up well. He had pulled his only suit out of hibernation, matched it to a tie that just managed to get away with being quirky and a pinstriped shirt she had never seen.

A present from one of his many ex-girlfriends, he had confided in her.

Classically, he just missed the mark, but he had the face of the perennial charmer. Wicked blue eyes and a rough appeal that had trapped many an unwary victim.

And she had taken time with her outfit as well. A smart, simple suit that was businesslike but in a warm apricot colour which stopped it from looking too severe. She knew that they looked like a well-matched team, but her heart was still beating madly when the time arrived and they were walking into the bar at the hotel.

A few days' reprieve and some sensible thinking had done very little to still her nerves. She found her eyes skittering around the room, searching him out. He wasn't there.

'Relax,' Jack said under his breath.

But even when they were seated, with their fruit juices in front of them, she still couldn't relax. She started to think he had changed his mind. His fiancée had talked him out of it and because she, Francesca, didn't matter, he hadn't seen fit to call and tell her the change of plan. By the time she finally saw his familiar figure standing in the doorway she had convinced herself that they were simply not going to bother to arrive.

Draped on his arm was a petite blonde, impeccably groomed and stunningly dressed in a casual short floral skirt and a silk vest top with a matching jacket that sat snugly on her waist. She heard Jack's swift intake of breath and smiled inwardly, imagining what he was thinking. Georgina would be just the sort of woman he found impossibly attractive. Blonde, small, fragile. He would find it very difficult not to flirt and, to his credit, he didn't. At least, not for the first forty-five minutes, during which they discussed menus, changes to menus, ingredients, everything under the sun to do with food.

All the while Francesca kept her eyes averted from Angelo, but every nerve in her body was tuned in to the lazy sprawl of his body on the chair next to her and to Georgina's hand, resting lightly and possessively on his wrist.

She didn't dare admit to herself how much it hurt to watch their familiarity, the way Georgina turned her face and smiled whenever he said anything, the way her slim hand sometimes touched his thigh in an absent-minded, feathery caress. She hoped to God she wasn't staring, but she knew that she was rigid with tension.

When a bottle of chilled wine was brought to their table, her weak refusal was ignored and Angelo poured her a glass and held it out for her. The slight brush of their fingers made her want to yank her hand back because it was as if an electric shock had been delivered to her body and, when her eyes met his, she could see from the cool smile on his face that he was well aware of her reaction.

'And how did you get into this line of business?' she heard Georgina ask Jack when most of the details had been discussed and Francesca was beginning to think that it was an appropriate time to leave.

'A very good question,' Angelo inserted conversationally. He leaned forward, elbows on knees, and gave Francesca the full benefit of his interest. 'A shared dream, perhaps?'

'Absolutely.' Jack grinned and stole a glance at her. 'Els—Franny lures them in with her amazing looks and I steal their hearts with my superb cooking.' He gazed at Georgina and raised his eyebrows mischievously.

'We share the cooking,' Francesca explained with a nervous smile. 'We also have a number of people who help us out when we're catering for larger parties.'

'And who are these people?' Georgina asked, directing her question to Jack.

'Usually from the catering school we use. Gives them experience. I'm a great believer in doing a good turn for someone else.' Francesca could tell without looking at him that his attention was all on the slight blonde and, judging from the delicate tinge in her cheeks, Georgina was blossoming under the masculine attention.

Angelo, she imagined, would be furious.

'I think it's time we left, Jack.' She smiled politely and tried to nudge her gregarious companion with her foot. 'Naturally we'll keep you informed of our progress and if perhaps you could let us know of any change to the numbers…?' So far, Jack had managed to steer away from personal conversation, but he was getting far too much into his element for her liking, quizzing Georgina on her tastes in food, treading a thin line between politeness and flirtation.

'Jack,' she said bluntly, turning to him, 'these people would perhaps like to leave and have some dinner. It's time we left.'

'Surely not quite yet. Angelo and I are riveted by your views on Continental cuisine. Have you travelled to all these faraway places that inspire you?'

Francesca all but groaned. Another bottle of wine was ordered. Jack, in full flow, discussed food with the aplomb of a gifted gourmet, sidestepped awkward questions and left her seething in her virtually non-alcoholic silence. Georgina, she noticed, was not averse to drinking her share and more. And Angelo…what was he thinking? His expression was shuttered. Was he thinking about taking his fiancée home? Making love to her? Being so close to him was unendurable agony because it reminded her of past times when she couldn't bear to be near him without wanting to tear his clothes off.

Georgina seemed absorbed in whatever Jack was now saying, but then, how different the situation was between her and Angelo. They probably lived together. Like normal people in love. That frantic coupling would not be part of their lifestyle. They could afford to enjoy each other's company without thinking of the absences looming on the horizon. Theirs would be a normal, happy life instead of periods spent apart, wishing the empty moments gone yet dreading the cruel passage of time.

Eventually, Francesca simply stood up and waited for Jack to follow suit. Georgina, she noticed, was swaying ever so slightly and her eyes were bright, too bright. She leaned in to Angelo and, as if taking a cue, Jack put his arm over Francesca's shoulder and gave her a brief squeeze.

'Looks like dinner might be off the cards,' Angelo said and Georgina stood on tiptoe and curled her hands around his neck. He gently untangled them but still supported her as they all left the bar, now busy with people.

Francesca didn't know if either was listening when she politely said goodbye, repeating all the usual platitudes about either she or Jack being in touch with them and, of course, do call if they had any problems.

She certainly wasn't listening to Jack as he waxed lyrical in the back of the taxi on the virtues of the delicate blonde. Seeing Angelo and Georgina had been just what she needed, a slap in the face and a long overdue end to all the nonsense she had been harbouring in her mind about unrequited love and a man pining for her.

She had been employed to do a job and she would do it well. Angelo Falcone might want to see her fail, but she wasn't going to let that happen and she wasn't going to let him affect her. The last thing she needed was for him to look down on her with pity and contempt from the splendid heights of his own domestic contentment.

The taxi dropped her off first. They lived within blocks of one another and, in fact, had, at points, debated the wisdom of sharing a house, but had both backed away from the idea. She didn't want the dubious pleasure of having to live with Jack's convoluted personal life and he, she suspected, did not want to run the risk of having her lecture him on his sloppy habits. So he continued to pay the rent on his property and she continued to pay her small mortgage, even though they saw one another daily.

The first thing Francesca did was to get rid of her suit, which she hung back up in her wardrobe, and have a shower. Then she slipped into some old jeans and an even older tee shirt and went into the kitchen to make herself something to eat. Years in the modelling world had made her very careful in her own eating habits and the fact that she dealt with food every day had made her very quick when it came to preparing anything for herself.

She was sitting down in front of a mushroom omelette and French bread when the doorbell rang.

This, she thought with irritation, was exactly when a butler would have been useful. *Jeeves, just tell Jack that I'm busy and, no, I won't be going with him to the pub for a quick drink.*

Instead, she padded across to the front door and opened it just enough of a crack to signal to Jack that she wasn't going out.

It wasn't Jack.

'Angelo! What are you doing here?' The chain on the door remained in place and she looked at him warily.

'Have I come at a bad time?'

'Inconvenient. I'm having my dinner.'

'I thought I might catch you both to apologise on behalf

of my fiancée.' He leaned against the door so that if she decided to close it she would find herself engaging in an undignified struggle.

'Jack's not here,' Francesca told him reluctantly. 'And if you lean any harder on this door you're going to break it.'

'That's the problem these days. Impossible to find solid craftsmanship anywhere. Are you going to let me in?'

'We've already discussed the food for your wedding.'

'I told you, I would like to apologise for Georgina. Humour me my good manners.'

No need to come in to apologise, she wanted to tell him. *You can do that quite easily from outside.* But he was her employer, at least for the time being. More importantly, he was someone who could ruin her if he so chose. And she was a professional. With a sigh, Francesca pulled the chain back and watched as he strolled into her house and looked around him with unconcealed curiosity.

It was a small, old semi-detached house but it had been refurbished to a very high standard. Gone were the dingy carpets. Instead, wooden floors had been laid throughout and the wallpaper had been replaced with various shades of paint, ranging from buff in the hallway to burgundy in the small dining room. The curtains were light and pooled on the ground and, in a burst of creative energy shortly after she had bought the house, Francesca had had installed a stained glass window which formed a dramatic partition between the dining room and the kitchen.

'Nice,' Angelo commented, taking it all in before allowing his eyes to rest on a now casually clad Francesca. 'Did you do it all yourself or did your boyfriend help?'

'You came to apologise, I believe?'

'It's something I do far better over a cup of coffee, or something stronger if you have it.'

Francesca sighed. 'You'd better come into the kitchen. I was in the middle of my dinner.'

'Smells good.'

'Angelo…' She paused and turned around to look at him. 'We had our chit-chat three days ago. And we had our serious talk about the menus today. So please spare me the polite conversation.' He obviously hadn't had time to completely change but the formal shirt had been replaced by a rugby style sweatshirt. He looked devastating. Too devastating for someone whose will-power had a tendency to flag whenever he was around. She could almost fill her nostrils with his clean, manly scent when she breathed in.

'Stop acting like a child, Francesca. There's nothing wrong with being polite. You seem to forget that I didn't purposefully seek you out.'

Francesca didn't reply. She stalked into the kitchen, looked at the mushroom omelette with distaste and made herself eat some of it while she waited for the kettle to boil.

When he sat opposite her, she resisted the temptation to tuck her knees to one side in case she touched him. Crazy! They had touched each other with hunger three years ago and yet now she couldn't bear to think of herself reacting to any inadvertent physical contact.

'I confess I was curious to meet your boyfriend. He wasn't what I was expecting.'

Francesca shrugged and pushed her plate to one side. 'What you were or weren't expecting is none of my business.' She made him his coffee, only belatedly realising that she had remembered how he took it. Strong, black, one sugar, just a level teaspoon. 'There's no need for you to apologise about your fiancée. It's easy to get a bit light-headed if you drink wine at that hour of the evening, before there's any food in your stomach. Was she pleased with what Jack and I had in mind for the meal? I hope so be-

cause last-minute changes are very difficult to accommodate.'

Angelo watched as she busied herself, tidying away
things from the kitchen counter, dumping dirty dishes in
the sink, doing anything to avoid looking at him. Talking
about anything but what he wanted to talk about—her partner. Jack was no ex-model, but they looked good together,
as though they belonged, and that had got to him. It enraged
him that this woman could still affect him after all these
absent years and after the way she had walked away from
their relationship.

He had dropped Georgina off, returned to his flat, semi-
changed, and decided that he was old enough and experienced enough not to allow his emotions to burst through
their restraints. Somehow, though, he had found himself
back at his car, had found himself punching in that address
on the business card into the Satellite Navigation finder in
his car, driving to her house.

'After years mixing with the glamorous people in the
modelling world, I was a little surprised to find that your
lover is…so…shall we say unapologetically lacking in polish?'

Francesca opened her mouth to refute the assumption
that Jack was her lover, and shut it.

'Maybe I find it refreshing to be with someone who isn't
impressed by what people do for a living or how much
money they earn.'

'Are you implying that I was?'

'I'm not implying anything.' But he was. Would he really have given her the time of day if she had been a checkout girl in a supermarket? And wasn't it telling that he had
ended up with a woman whose pedigree would be a credit
to him?

'How long have you known him?'

'A while.'

'A while being…?'

'Being none of your business, Angelo. In fact, my life is none of your business. I can't take away the fact that we were once an item, but that was then and this is now.' She was leaning against the sink, arms folded, every muscle tense.

'Which doesn't mean that I don't still have your interests at heart.' He liked the sound of that. Liked the way it made him rise above the pettiness of jealousy into the higher realms of magnanimity.

Francesca snorted with open disbelief. 'And how do you work that one out, Angelo? How have you gone from wanting to settle old scores to caring about my personal welfare?'

'I admit when I first saw you it brought a lot of old feelings out into the open. I am only human, after all,' Angelo drawled. 'But since then I've realised that I owe it to you to be honest and I honestly cannot see what you find stimulating about him.'

'And that's why you came? Because you're big-hearted and you just wanted to express concern about my choice of partner?' She looked at him resentfully, not liking the way he had come into her house and taken it over. 'I love Jack,' she said truthfully. 'We work together and we get along well.' She shrugged. 'It doesn't bother me that he's *unapologetically lacking in polish*, as you put it. Actually, I think it's pretty superficial to judge someone on their appearance. It's what's underneath that counts. But I don't suppose you would agree with that.' She knew that this was a pointless conversation. She knew that she should be as polite but as distant as she could be with him, remind herself that he was a man due to be married to a woman he was in love with. But seeing him after all this time out of the blue had turned her world upside down and she could feel herself hurtling towards an argument, any argument.

'Because I'm such a superficial person?' He shot her a tight, cold smile. 'I don't remember you accusing me of that particular trait three years ago.'

'You went out with a model,' Francesca retorted. 'That says it all.'

'In other words, you consider yourself to have been superficial and shallow then. Is that it?'

'I was glamorous and you went for the glamour.'

'And your boyfriend didn't? Look in the mirror, Francesca. You might no longer dress in skimpy designer outfits and strut down catwalks, but you've still got the same face and the same body. You might think that packing in the modelling job and going down the sensible career route has suddenly turned you into Ms Averagely Good-Looking whose mind turns men's heads, but let me assure you that the way you look is still going to be what ropes them in.' He allowed the insult time to ferment before going on. 'And, once you've roped them in, who knows how long the attraction will last? You cannot have failed to notice that your lover was paying more attention than was strictly polite to my fiancée…'

So that was what this visit was about, she thought. He hadn't come to apologise about Georgina's slightly tipsy introduction to them, nor had he come in the role of big-hearted Mr Kind who wanted to save her from her incompatibility with Jack. He had come because he had noticed Jack's flirting. It hadn't been obvious, but then Angelo was a man who noticed the most subtle of nuances.

'That's not true!' Francesca said quickly. 'He's just very friendly, very outgoing, very charming.'

'So outgoing and charming that he barely looked at you

once during the entire time we were sitting at that table?'
He laughed as though she had taken leave of her senses.

'We weren't on a date. Of course he wasn't going to sit
and stare at me with big infatuated eyes!' She could feel
patches of bright colour on her cheeks. 'We were there to
do a job and, since we'll probably be dealing mostly with
your fiancée, of course he's going to try and form a bond,
make sure that they can communicate!' Who was she kid-
ding? Underneath all the perfectly courteous chit-chat, Jack
had pulled the ladies' man out of the drawer. She had detected it in the modulation of his voice and the husky note
of his laughter which, she now reflected, there had been far
too much of. Georgina hadn't cracked any thigh-slapping
jokes and her coy remarks certainly hadn't deserved the
level of amusement they had received.

'You have no idea how difficult it is catering for someone when there's a personality clash,' she forged ahead
valiantly.

'And how much easier when your lover can charm and
flirt his way into his client's affections, hmm? Is this a
double act you two have perfected? I imagine it works a
treat with the golden oldies too.'

'Don't be sordid,' Francesca said sharply. 'If Jack's manner was out of place, then I apologise on his behalf. So
we're quits. Two apologies that cancel each other out.' She
pushed herself away from the counter and was heading for
the kitchen door when his hand snapped out and caught her
wrist.

The touch galvanized her body into immediate shameful
response. She clenched her fist and it was all she could do
to maintain a normal voice.

'I'm not finished yet,' Angelo said smoothly. He could
feel the slight tremble running through her body straight

into his. It was shockingly energising, and very satisfying. Lover or no lover, he still got to her.

He had to shake himself with the reminder that he was a man engaged to be married. As quickly as he had grabbed her wrist, he now dropped it.

'I don't know what to say.' Francesca clasped her arms to her chest and kept her head averted, talking to the door, although she could feel his eyes boring into her. 'I know you're probably angry but, like I said, Jack is a sociable animal. There would have been nothing intentional in his behaviour towards your fiancée.'

'Would you like to look at me when you say that or is it easier to say when you're turned away?'

Francesca looked at him. 'He's a really nice guy, Angelo. I'm sorry if you think he was flirting with Georgina, but he wouldn't.'

'Because he's so committed to you?'

'I know you want to hurt me, Angelo, but don't bring Jack into it. Don't ruin what we've built up. Jack's worked hard for this and it hasn't been easy for him.'

'What do you mean by that?'

Francesca could have kicked herself. He had detected something in her voice and he was all ears now.

'I mean that…that he's had to…sacrifice earning while he was doing his catering course…and…'

'Don't tell me that you didn't support him financially. With all that cash you'd managed to tuck away over the years?' He looked at her with a shuttered expression. Something wasn't making sense but, whatever connection he was missing, he couldn't locate it. 'Trying to buy his love, Francesca?'

'What do you mean?'

'You might be able to pull the purse-strings but if your man has a wandering eye then he's always going to have a wandering eye. You might think that you're calling the shots, but what's he up to when your back's turned?'

Since she knew exactly what Jack was up to when her back was turned she could afford to smile at that misconception. 'I know what he's up to.' Chatting up women and having random affairs, because when it came to relationships the slightest hint of commitment was enough to send him hurtling off in the opposite direction. Her only advice to him was to practise safe sex. Beyond that, he was on his own.

Angelo didn't like the answer. 'And you don't care?'

'He's not up to anything that I disapprove of.' Her voice was steadier now that she was on safe ground and she was no longer trembling. But he was still in her house and there was no way she could relax with him sitting there, inches away from her. She glanced meaningfully at the front door, just visible from where she was standing.

Angelo stood up and she licked her lips nervously. She was tall but she had always felt physically dwarfed by him and it was even more apparent here, in the small kitchen, with the atmosphere crackling between them.

'Very trusting. Very optimistic.'

'And what about you?' she flung at him. She threw her head back and stared up into those black, fathomless eyes. 'If you noticed Jack flirting with your fiancée you must have noticed that she wasn't exactly pushing him away in horror!' Damned if he was going to stride into her house and issue smug, patronising generalisations on the quality of her love life as if she was a halfwit incapable of making the correct choices. 'So what have you got to say to that?'

CHAPTER FOUR

'I'M SORRY. That was out of order.' Francesca backed out of the kitchen and turned away, walking quickly towards the front door, anxious to get him out of her house, even more anxious to curtail a dangerous conversation that had her teetering between a recognition that she had to be polite and a yearning to draw blood.

'Tricky, isn't it?' Angelo drawled, strolling towards her and then propping himself up with one hand on the door, making sure that she couldn't actually open it.

'What is?'

'Pretending.'

'Pretending what? I'm not pretending anything!' Her voice was laced with panic.

'Oh, yes, you are,' he chided softly. 'We both are. Pretending that the past is over and done with and we no longer give a damn about what happens in each other's lives…'

'I *don't* give a damn what happens in yours!' Francesca finally raised her eyes and looked at him. She found herself mesmerised by his mouth. She imagined it touching hers and she had to fight the convulsive shudder that threatened to rip through her. '*You're* the one who keeps referring to our past! I'm just interested in getting on with this job and doing it to the best of my ability!'

'Oh, really. And do you normally tremble like a leaf when you're in the company of one of your male clients? Because you're trembling now.'

'I'm nervous!' Francesca cried. 'You make me nervous!'

'Why?'

'You know why! Because you're right. A few well-placed words could ruin what Jack and I have built up!' A few well-placed words could do a hell of a lot more damage than that, but there was no way she was going to let him have any insights into her thoughts and fears.

'And what if I give you my word that I will do nothing to endanger your livelihood?' He realised that he didn't want her tiptoeing around him, scared to death that he might carry out his casual threat. Not that he knew what he wanted. He shook his head in exasperation. 'I have no intention of ruining you, Francesca. I admire what you've done. It must have taken a lot of guts to walk away from a safe income and take a chance on something like catering. And you, who never knew how to boil an egg.' He raised his eyebrows and smiled at her, the first genuine smile she had seen on his face since fate had brought them back together.

Guarded though she remained, she felt herself relax. Just a little. Enough to return a ghost of a smile.

'I know.' When she lowered her eyes she saw his firm, sensual mouth. Lower them a bit more and she bumped into the hard expanse of his chest.

He was right. It was tricky pretending, acting as though they were vague acquaintances who just happened to have bumped into one another. A lot of the friction between them could be eradicated if they could speak to one another normally. She drew in a deep breath and looked at him.

'Would you like another coffee, Angelo? I apologise if I've been on edge. It's been hard wondering whether you were going to pull the rug from under our feet...'

Our feet. The coupling involved in that simple phrase cut him to the quick. It was a reaction he kept to himself as he took hold of the olive branch offered and accepted the coffee, obliging her by going into the sitting room to wait while she made it.

The sitting room was as modern as the rest of the house. Comfortable, with a deep sofa and two generously sized chairs, but there were no concessions to the Victorian origins of the house. The rug was thick and boldly inviting while the walls, bar two dramatic framed posters, were free of clutter.

She walked in while he was inspecting the room and quietly placed the coffee on the squat side table by the sofa, then she sat on one of the chairs and watched him.

'I always imagined that you would be drawn to the little country house with the white picket fence,' he said finally, looking at her over the rim of his cup as he sipped.

'One day.' Francesca shrugged. 'Just not yet. London is the right place to be when it comes to catering. Much bigger catchment area. I could still do it in the country somewhere, but I doubt there would be enough money in it to keep things going and I can't afford to try and turn a hobby into a living.'

'So where did the money go, Francesca?'

'Houses in London aren't cheap and especially houses in a halfway decent location.'

'So all those earnings went into buying this place?'

'Mostly.' She lowered her eyes, knowing that he would have clocked into the obvious discrepancy. She *had* been a successful model for quite a while and the pay cheques had not been measly. 'And also there's the purpose-built kitchen behind the house. If we wanted to do catering seriously we couldn't just make do with my tiny kitchen. I had to have that built and it wasn't cheap.'

'And what does the boyfriend contribute to this scenario? What was he doing before he went into cooking?'

It was a perfectly harmless question. Francesca tried not

to read criticism into it but she could feel her hackles rise and she swallowed down the urge to launch into another defensive argument. There was no mileage in arguing with Angelo. It just created a never-ending atmosphere of thick tension in which it was impossible to function. Bad enough sitting here with him, in the same room, knowing that only a few metres of empty space separated them.

He was leading the way by behaving in an adult fashion with her and it was her duty to follow his lead. She drew in a deep breath and skirted around a potentially perilous question.

'He was doing this and that. You know. Well, actually, you probably don't. I can't imagine you were ever someone who just did this and that.'

'I admit I never saw the value of wasting time trying out a few occupations for size before settling on the right one. Life is too short for wrong turnings.' The only wrong turning he had ever made in his life had involved the woman sitting across the room from him now. She had the face of an angel and, for a moment in time, he had thought she had the personality to match. She hadn't. She had wanted him, desired him, tantalised him, but she had never seen a future in him. He had made a huge error of judgement with her and he felt bitterly proud that he could be sitting here, conducting a conversation with her for all the world as though they had parted on good terms.

It was, he told himself, a mark of his self-control that he had managed to subdue the basic urge for revenge that had blinded him when he had unexpectedly set eyes on her a few days ago. Not only that, but he could engage in conversation about her lover. Of course, it helped that he had Georgina.

He realised guiltily that his fiancée hadn't crossed his mind once since entering the house.

'Sometimes you need to take a few wrong turnings before you find the right one,' Francesca said, thinking of all the wrong turnings she had taken in her past.

'Are you referring to us?' Angelo asked silkily and she flushed.

'No, of course not!'

'Then what? Your past? A time before you met me?'

'No,' she said quickly. 'You're right. I was referring to us. I mean, here you are now, engaged to be married. It's wonderful!' She gave a high, brittle laugh. 'And Georgina is just right for you, Angelo.'

'In what way?'

'Well, she's beautiful and well-educated and...sophisticated...'

'And you were none of those things?'

'We're not talking about me.' The little lies she had told came back in a rush. The non-existent education, and her sophistication had been of the purely surface sort. A few scratches and under the glitter was the hard, ugly metal. Not that he had ever known that. 'How did you meet her?' she asked, changing the subject.

'At a party given by mutual friends.'

Francesca could picture the scene. A collection of glamorous, well-bred people, the elite of the elite. She could imagine Angelo's reaction when he saw the small blonde, the awakening of sudden, intense passion, the pursuit. She had lived it and loved it for a short while.

'You must be very excited at the prospect of getting married.'

'The time is right.' He shrugged and sipped some of the coffee. 'There is no need to look so aghast, Francesca. Don't tell me that you still believe in love and romance?'

'As a matter of fact, I do.'

'And it's what you have found with your boyfriend? Love, romance and the promise of a fairytale ending?'

'What's wrong with that?' Francesca lowered her eyes. It crossed her mind that the small deceit about her relationship with Jack, initiated for all the right reasons, might not have been such a great idea after all. She now had no choice but to go along for the ride.

Angelo felt a sharp, brief stab of jealousy and smiled coolly. 'Nothing if you happen to have your head in the clouds. You're right. Georgina and I are well-matched. She is all that any man could want in a wife, a perfect foil for me, as a matter of fact.'

'Meaning what?'

'Meaning that she detests confrontations as much as I do. I find that an admirable trait in a woman. Makes for a very harmonious atmosphere.'

'Makes for a doormat, if you ask me,' Francesca muttered under her breath, and he leaned forward, straining to hear.

'I don't think I caught that.'

'I just wondered whether a marriage in which there are absolutely no confrontations might be a little unchallenging for a man like you, Angelo.'

Same old indifference to his boundaries, he noted angrily. He opened his mouth to put her neatly in her place, but she had already taken up the threads of her observation.

'I mean, isn't it going to get a little boring if you spend all your time in the company of someone who only knows how to agree with you? Face it, it's hardly as though you don't have a huge repertoire of very contentious ideas.' She laughed, ignoring the stunned displeasure on his face.

'Are you telling me that I am making a mistake with my fiancée?' Angelo enquired coldly, and Francesca's laughter faded away.

'No, of course not! I'm sure Georgina isn't as submissive as you pretend.'

'And maybe I have learnt after my experiences with you that I prefer women who do not disrespect me.'

Francesca accepted the inflammatory criticism in mortified silence. Yes, she had broken off their relationship. He had wanted more of her—but he hadn't proposed, had he? He had saved that for the right woman.

'Then lucky you. You found someone who fits the bill,' she replied blandly. She stood up. 'I'm really tired, Angelo. It's been nice chatting to you.' She walked towards the door and waited in the doorway for him, both hands pressed behind her. 'It's good that we can both be adults.' He was standing right in front of her now and she felt her mouth go dry.

'Isn't it. You're trembling again, Francesca. Don't tell me that I still make you nervous, even though I've reassured you that I won't be making any efforts to discredit you. In fact, if your food lives up to its promise I'll be sure to recommend you to friends and clients.'

Was she trembling? 'Thank you. We can always use all the help we can get and word of mouth is the best form of advertising in this business.' The words were coming out but her brain felt like cotton wool. All she could see was the even rise and fall of his broad chest.

Angelo reached out and feathered his finger along her arm. It was barely a touch but still enough to send her nervous system into immediate meltdown. She pressed herself harder against the doorframe to stop herself from sliding ignominiously to the ground.

'Have you wondered, Francesca?' he asked softly.

'Wondered? Wondered what?'

'Wondered what it would be like to make love again…'

'No, I have not! And that's…that's…*disgusting*! You're

engaged to be married, Angelo! I realise that you might be cynical about love and romance but don't you have any loyalty *at all*?'

'There's no need to get so morally outraged.' He smiled at her with lazy amusement. 'I wasn't proposing that we rip our clothes off and have sex in your hallway.'

Francesca squeaked and Angelo raised his eyebrows. 'You didn't think that, did you? As you said, that was then and this is now.'

'I…I…' she spluttered.

'I wouldn't cheat on my fiancée. Which isn't to say that my mind has not speculated on what we had. We *were* very good together in bed, after all…'

'Your mind…your mind should behave itself, Angelo! And it's not right that we should be talking about this!'

'I thought we had done away with the pretending game.'

'It's time for you to go.'

'Meaning that this conversation embarrasses you?'

'Meaning that this conversation is inappropriate. What would Georgina say if she knew…knew…?'

'That we once had an affair? I doubt she would mind. Thankfully, she's not the jealous type.'

'I would be,' Francesca muttered.

'Then you and your boyfriend must have had quite a row after his flirtatious behaviour this evening.'

'I told you, Jack wasn't flirting.'

'Then you're not very clever at reading body language.'

Not very clever at reading body language? She was reading her body language now and she didn't like what it was saying. Every fibre of her was pulsing, reacting to him. Her breasts felt tender and her nipples were pushing painfully against her bra. He could still do this to her even though she could feel his three-year-old anger simmering just beneath the surface.

'And *you* weren't jealous, Angelo? I don't believe that! Even if you tell me that you don't believe in love and romance, you forget that I know you! You used to question every male model I had to do a shoot with!'

'Fortunately since then I've learnt to use my head when it comes to women,' Angelo grated. He opened his mouth to say something but she would never know because just then the doorbell rang. Literally saved by the bell.

She darted towards the door, breathing unevenly, and opened it to find that her saviour was Jack.

'He's here!' she hissed under her breath, grabbing him by the collar of his shirt and tugging him closer to her.

'And he's getting under your skin. Interesting.'

'This is no time to joke, Jack. Just…just put your arms around me and do a convincing act of being my boyfriend, would you?'

With his arms around her, she felt safe from the coal-black eyes burning a hole behind her and, by the time she had unwrapped herself from the embrace, she was more or less back in control.

Angelo had finally taken the hint she had been giving him ever since he'd first stepped through her door earlier on and was ready to leave. He nodded briefly at Jack and then looked coolly at Francesca, who was presenting a united front with Jack pressed next to her.

'I'll be in touch.'

'Of course.' She smiled but her jaw ached. It was a relief when he closed the door quietly behind him and her tense muscles could sag.

'You're going to have to deal with him from now on, Jack.' She headed towards the kitchen, knowing that he would follow and that he would also sense her mood and get her a cup of coffee while she sat at the table and tried to recover from feeling as though she had been mown down by a steamroller.

'Do you want to jack the job in?' He handed her a cup of coffee and sat at the opposite end of the table.

Weird, she thought, that he would be the one caretaking her now, when it had always been the other way around. Time certainly changed everything. His bad old days had gone. She felt as though hers were now about to begin and a wave of resentment flooded through her at the thought that Angelo could step back into her life and manage to turn it upside down.

'And sacrifice my pride? Let us both down?' She laughed shortly. 'I don't think so.' Then, on a sigh, 'But he's playing with me, Jack. *Let's behave like adults and civilised adults can discuss the past without getting emotional.* And he enjoys watching me when I react. He never used to be like that, like a cat toying with a mouse. He said he doesn't intend to use his influence to our disadvantage and I believe him, but he's happy to watch my discomfort every time I'm around him.'

'And you're uncomfortable because…? Why don't you just tell him the truth?'

'No.' Why not? Because she didn't want to watch the scales drop from his eyes. He might hate her for walking out on him, but if he saw her in all her honest glory he would be contemptuous and she didn't want that. Her pride again, but then who didn't have an abundance of that particular vice? 'No, the answer is for you to deal with him. There's no reason for him to call in a hurry, anyway. He doesn't have the excuse of wanting to go through menus or anything like that and he's not going to interrupt his work schedule to make pointless contact with us just because he likes watching me squirm in his presence.'

'Then you don't have anything to worry about.' He

dragged a chair over with one foot and settled into a more comfortable position. 'So you can sit there and listen about me. You haven't even asked why I turned up here when I should have been down at the pub…'

His convoluted story of an enraged husband—'Never suspected a thing,'—a child in the background—'I'll never trust a blonde again,'—and a pleading woman—'I told her from the start that I was all about the Fun,'—more or less managed to take her mind off the problem preying on it like a lethal virus with a mission to destroy. But as soon as Jack had left, walking back to his place after a couple of beers, she was thinking again about Angelo, replaying everything he had said to her.

She couldn't believe that after all this time, and after all the changes she had made in her life, she could still find herself hurtling back into the past with such a lack of self-control. Back there, in the sitting room, when he had been standing in front of her deliberately baiting her with memories of when they were lovers, she had felt her body melting. Yes, he had been goading her on. Yes, he had liked seeing her rigid with discomfort. Yes, yes, yes! But she had still responded, against her will, against all rhyme and reason, and it had been written all over her face. No wonder he had been so insolently dismissive of her so-called relationship with Jack.

The intervening week gave her plenty of time to brood over the unfolding scenario. In fact, it became a close companion as she went through the books, paid a visit to their bank manager, dealt with the steady flow of clients and their demands. Daily stress had now linked hands with simmering panic and, between the two, they were giving her a number of reasons to lose sleep.

Jack, of course, was once again blithely sauntering through life, cooking magnificently in the kitchen, experimenting with different combinations and nurturing a new relationship which, he assured her, was free of hidden complications. He should know. He had cunningly checked out her house for contradictory signals, which apparently had been his big mistake with Jodie, the Blonde with the Background.

His amusing stories at least managed to keep her on an even keel. Thank God for him! He invited her to have opinions on everything, from his cooking to his love life, never leaving her the option of slinking quietly into her own thoughts and getting overwhelmed by them. Nor did he press her to share them with him.

She had to wait until she was in bed to really indulge in the nightmare of having Angelo around. If only she had never been recommended to Georgina. If only she had not been greedy and decided that they could handle a really big job. If only, if only.

But then, something whispered in her head, don't you feel *alive* for the first time in years? That always seemed to be the little voice that had the last whisper before she fell asleep and was the first to greet her when she woke up in the morning.

But as the days dragged on and the phone remained thankfully free of Angelo's dark, disturbing voice, she felt herself begin to relax a bit more.

She had been right. There was no need for contact, at least not for a while, not until they needed to make practical arrangements for delivery of the food. They would have to discuss what staff Angelo and Georgina needed and what staff they were going to employ themselves for an event of that size. There was nothing to be gained in mentally rehearsing conversations that would take place down the line and the grind of daily life left her little time to add that further element of stress to the repertoire already there and thriving.

So she didn't think about it. In fact, she so successfully convinced herself that he was a distant bridge that she could happily defer crossing until some unspecified time in the future that it was a shock when, on a balmy Saturday evening, she answered the phone and heard his voice down the line.

She sat down as her stomach took an immediate nose-dive, quickly followed by the rest of her internal organs.

'What are you doing?' was the first thing he asked her, before she had time to get her head in order.

'What am I doing when?'

'Now.'

'Now? I'm…I'm…well…'

'Nothing,' he inserted helpfully. 'Good. Because I've decided to pay you a little visit.'

'It's nearly six-thirty, Angelo! Jack and I…have plans…'

'Have you? That's funny. I telephoned him at his house. You remember his number is also on your business card? Someone called Robbie answered and informed me that he's house-sitting for the weekend because Jack's somewhere in Yorkshire until Monday. You mean you didn't know?' Angelo clicked his tongue sympathetically. 'Very bad to be kept in the dark about your boyfriend's movements…'

Yorkshire. The wretched cricket match which he had been determined to see with his mates.

'Oh, yes,' she said weakly. 'Now I remember.'

'So I thought that I would rescue you from an evening of solitude.'

'Don't you have more pressing plans for a Saturday night?'

'Georgina is…not around, shall we say? So I'll be with

you in, say, half an hour. We're going to go and buy some food and then you are going to show me what you can do with it.'

'Jack is the real genius when it comes to the food,' Francesca wittered on as a sickening alternative to Saturday night in presented itself. 'I'm the lackey, really. Chopping and stuff.'

'Chopping's a good start. And don't put yourself down, Francesca. I have every faith in your talents and I'm curious to see what you can produce. I will see you shortly.'

He seemed to have become very talented at abrupt conversations because he didn't give her time to voice any more objections. In fact, he barely gave her time to brush her hair and stick on some make-up and then the doorbell was ringing and there he was. Cool, casual and impossibly good-looking. And on her doorstep. And yes, she was horrified to see him standing there. But she was also... shamefully excited.

'I've already brought the wine.' He handed her two bottles of very expensive stuff which she dumped on the table in the hallway before grabbing her bag.

'This is just crazy.' Her heart was thumping madly as she looked at him. He was wearing a casual pair of cream trousers and an open-necked designer polo shirt. Against it, his skin was bronzed and vitally attractive and she didn't want to stare so she focused on the logo on his shirt instead.

'What's wrong with crazy some of the time?' Crazy? It didn't feel crazy to him. It felt like the sanest thing he had done in a while. Georgina, he mused, would have been very hard pressed to agree with his self-diagnosis. She, too, had called him crazy when he had spoken to her three days before. A lot else, as well. In fact, crazy had been one of her more gentle remarks.

'You can't do this,' she had told him, over her spritzer

in his apartment. 'You can't just *break off this engagement*, not when everything's been planned and invitations have been sent out!'

But after the tears and the pleading had come the inevitable rage. And, at that stage, crazy had been one of her less flamboyant descriptions of him.

Angelo had gritted his teeth and sat through the tirade. He had felt sorry for her, in a curiously detached way, but had been implacable in his decision and he knew that his implacability had fuelled her anger, as had his observation that she would find someone far more suitable as a husband in time.

He had been relieved when she had finally stormed out of his apartment, after informing him that she would be keeping the vastly expensive diamond engagement ring and that he could cover the costs of every single thing that could not be returned. It had seemed a very small price to pay, in his opinion.

The only thing he had kept from her had been the reason why he had decided not to go through with the marriage. That would have been honesty stretched to the point of needless cruelty, so he had mentioned nothing of his previous relationship with their caterer and had greeted accusations of infidelity in complete silence.

'Do you mean,' Francesca was saying as she struggled to divest herself of the idea that they were *on a date* and focus on the notion that he might just want to prove to himself that she could cook, 'that you're testing my skills? For the big day? Just in case I secretly use cook-in sauces in my recipes? I don't, as it happens.'

'I'm glad to hear it. So you won't mind proving it to me. My car's just there so we'll drive to the nearest supermarket. Where is it?'

'I usually get my fresh meat and fish directly from

source,' Francesca said with a touch of pride. 'And the meat is always organic.'

'Well, I think that just for tonight we will do away with the fish and meat markets and just take what we can get at the supermarket counters. I can take or leave the organic business.'

'That's not a very twenty-first century response,' Francesca said, slipping into the passenger seat and watching her house disappear with a certain amount of foreboding.

'Well, maybe I am not a very twenty-first century man.' He shifted down a gear at the traffic lights and glanced sideways at her. She was making a point of not looking at him but she would look at him eventually. There was no rush. He felt the same warm satisfaction spread through him as he had felt earlier on in the week, when he had made the decision to break off his engagement and to do what his gut instincts had been telling him he needed to do from the very first time he had set eyes on her in that restaurant in Covent Garden. He was no twenty-first century man.

Telling himself that he was civilised enough to restrict his responses to a casual shrug over an unfortunate episode in his past had been a vast misjudgement of his own character. His relationship with her had never, for him, been casual enough to warrant such indifference.

Revenge was an ugly notion, and no, he was not out to get revenge. He needed to remove her from his system and the only way he could achieve that, he had realised in one of his brutally honest moments, would be to have her once again. The fact that she was involved with someone else was an irritating technicality. As far as he was concerned, she and Jack were a ridiculous and improbable match and he would be doing her a favour by divesting her of that particular relationship.

The thought that Jack might once have been a rival on the side would make it all the sweeter.

He would have her and then, when it suited him and suit him it would, he would dismiss her but at least she would cease to haunt him. He would not consider her feelings because, as she would be the first to agree, surely, wasn't all fair in love and war?

The wheel, at last, would turn full circle and it would be a thoroughly enjoyable process. Better still, he would be the one steering it.

'What sort of meal do you have in mind?' Francesca asked, breaking into his pleasurable train of thought, and he shot her a brief glance.

'Something interesting involving fish and chicken,' he said. 'You're the expert. What would you advise?'

Francesca looked at him suspiciously. He seemed in remarkably high spirits considering she was the one in the passenger seat.

'I could do prawns in garlic for starters. It's pretty simple and quick to do. And then, I suppose, chicken with green olives and we could have that with fresh pasta. I do know how to make my own pasta but I won't have the time to do that.'

Maybe another day, he was inclined to say.

'Do you limit yourself to Italian cooking in your catering?' he asked, slowing down as they approached the supermarket on their left.

'Why are you being so nice to me, Angelo?'

'So suspicious, Francesca. I wouldn't want to rub you up the wrong way and discover that the secret ingredient in my food was a touch of arsenic, would I?'

Francesca felt her mouth twitch in amusement but there was no way that she was going to indulge his sense of humour. She was suspicious and she had every right to be in view of his attitude towards her since they had met again. She had a sudden, vivid memory of the laughter they used to share. His wit had always extended beyond amusing surface charm. He could be funny enough to have her holding her sides. She shut the door firmly on that memory.

'I'm fresh out of arsenic, as it happens, and I don't believe it's stocked in supermarkets.'

Angelo grinned and manoeuvred his car into one of the free parking spaces. 'So I'm safe for now. Good. Life is…sweet at the moment. I wouldn't—' he killed the engine and turned to her '—want to give it up just yet.'

Francesca suddenly realised just how small the confines of his car were and she felt a lick of nervousness.

'You haven't answered my question. Why are you being so nice?'

'Let's just say…' his black eyes locked on hers '…that I have discovered all sorts of challenges where there were none before. A very exciting prospect to a jaded soul like mine.' He smiled slowly and Francesca, suddenly drowning in nectar, opened her car door and shot out.

Challenges? What challenges? Something to do with work, she supposed. He had once told her that the compulsion to work was driven not for love of money, or status, or power, but for the excitement of closing a difficult deal.

If not work, then maybe he was beginning to truly appreciate the anticipation of his impending marriage and the challenges that would inevitably offer.

It didn't matter. She didn't want to waste time unravelling his enigmatic statement. What she wanted was to cook him his meal, prove herself capable of the job they had given her and get him out of her house.

CHAPTER FIVE

AS PLANS went it was fine but its execution got off to a grindingly slow start. Francesca, having had the trolley manoeuvred out of her grasp, was inclined to circumnavigate the Saturday evening crowds and do the equivalent of a trolley dash. She very rarely browsed in supermarkets. She came with a long list, usually shopped during antisocial hours and always bought what had to be bought in record time.

Angelo, on the other hand, appeared to be in no rush. The first five minutes found him thumbing through the CDs on sale just beyond the rows of magazines by the huge opening doors.

He could feel her steaming behind him and let his fingers travel along the rack of CDs, pulling out another one and reading the index of songs at super slow speed.

'What,' he asked, turning to her, 'do you think of this one? I live over here now, but regrettably I have not managed to get into the music.' He handed her the CD and watched as she impatiently scanned it.

'Have you any intention of buying a CD?' Francesca asked. 'I thought we came in here to buy food so that I could cook you a meal and prove that I'm capable of meeting your standards.' She handed him back the CD and folded her arms.

Dressed casually, she was even more of a knockout than in the neatly tailored suits he had seen her in previously. Her jeans were faded to the palest of blues and fitted her like a second skin, flaring slightly at the bottom, revealing

79

slender feet tucked into workmanlike sandals that would have looked ungainly on any other woman. Models, even ex-models, were built to be put into anything and still look good. Francesca was no exception. Where she differed was that she carried just sufficient weight to look feminine, even though her expression now was anything but.

Undeterred, Angelo surveyed her blandly, although he could feel the adrenaline pumping through him at the thought of his seduction and its inevitable success. A part of him marvelled at the fact that less than a week previously he had been engaged to be married to someone else. Of course, he had always known that he had chosen Georgina because of her credentials, had known that his fondness for her had never extended to love, had willingly accepted that her own feelings for him had been wrapped up in the tremendous ego boost of having landed someone as eminently eligible as he was...but, amazingly, he had given her no more than a passing thought since he had broken off their engagement.

Would he tell Francesca of that little development? he wondered.

Or would he bed her knowing that even the thought of him being betrothed to another woman would not be enough for her to resist him? How fitting for her to plead for him when she had once walked away.

'We need music to listen to while we eat,' he said, infuriatingly turning round to reach for another CD. At this rate, Francesca worked out that they wouldn't make it to the fresh meat section before closing time.

'I have music.' She relieved him of what he was holding and pointedly returned it to the rack.

'But do you have music that I would like?'

'Well, since you haven't got into English music you'll just have to trust my taste. Okay? Because we can't dawdle here for hours sifting through CDs. You want me to cook for you—fine. I mean, it's not something any other client has ever requested...'

'But then, I am unique,' Angelo pronounced with such staggering arrogance that Francesca raised her eyes skywards and sighed elaborately. 'Okay, okay.' He raised both hands in mock surrender. 'I'll trust your taste in music and we'll get down to the business of buying food.'

And no chat. It was the message he was reading loud and clear from her body language. He let her have it her way for the first ten minutes, obediently looking on in silence while she frowned over the cuts of meat and inspected the vegetables for freshness.

Supermarket shopping was not something Angelo did on a regular basis, or any kind of basis for that matter. He had a housekeeper who took care of keeping his fridge stocked up and, if he ever needed anything beyond the usual, he simply took himself off to the nearest delicatessen and paid over the odds for the privilege. And, of course, for the past few months Georgina had cooked for him, basic English food that was unadventurous but edible.

For a short while he was content to eye the shelves and watch Francesca at work. Just for a short while, though.

'Tell me what sort of music you like listening to,' he said while she was frowning over the fresh pasta, and Francesca jumped because suddenly he was a lot closer to her than she had thought.

'Why?'

'Because I am interested.' Sinfully black eyes roamed over her face, taking in her consternation. So desperate to keep him at arms' length. Because of Jack? Something was missing from that relationship, whatever she said about love and perfect bonding, but he couldn't quite work out what. Still, in his head, Jack was no longer a rival. In fact, he was fast becoming a ghost so he stifled the surge of jealousy and smiled sincerely at her.

'In Venice, we always used to listen to classical music. Do you remember?' He took a packet of fresh tagliatelle from the chilled counter and tossed it into the trolley, then he began weaving slowly towards the aisles of tinned food. Much quieter there. He paused and spent an inordinately long time staring at various sauces while she stood hesitantly next to him and wondered what to say.

'Somehow that always felt right in Venice. It's a classical music sort of place.'

'It never occurred to me that you might actually dislike that kind of music…'

'I don't.'

'So tell me what you will be playing for us tonight over our wonderful meal, hmm?'

Francesca forced herself not to be rattled at his determination to chat to her. It was only natural. After all, they could hardly walk round a supermarket in total silence or else spend the entire evening conversing on the subject of food, fascinating though that was. There was just so much anyone could find to say about the merits of fresh shaved parmesan cheese over the mass produced grated variety. He was chatting because by nature he was an adept social mixer.

If she was jittery then it was entirely her fault. She couldn't seem to stop him affecting her.

'I have quite a good jazz collection.' She guided the trolley away from the pointless jars and towards the checkout tills.

'Not exactly new and modern, though, is it?'

'You'd hate new and modern, Angelo.' The queues were long. Francesca could see the woman in front glancing surreptitiously at Angelo, probably trying to work out whether he was famous, whether she should recognise him.

'Try me.'

'I think you're confusing me with your fiancée. Shouldn't she be the one opening you up to the joys of modern English music?'

Angelo's eyes became veiled. 'Georgina only does easy listening. Oh, and classical, of course, because that has always been my preferred taste.'

'And, naturally, she would never want to have an opinion on anything that contradicts her lord and master.' Flustered at the outburst, Francesca stared down into the trolley and took a deep, calming breath. 'Sorry. Out of order and, before you ask, no, I'm not saying that you two aren't suited. But you have to admit that it's a bit strange. You coming to my house, getting me to cook for you. I can't help but think that Georgina wouldn't be exactly over the moon at that, and I don't care how many un-jealous bones she's got in her body.' She looked at him seriously and lowered her voice. 'You must know that you're putting me in a very uncomfortable position just by hiring me to cater for your wedding, never mind this—you being here. Is that why you've come? Because you enjoy seeing me uncomfortable?'

'You are being paranoid.' He had forgotten how much he liked the way she stripped all the outer layers from a conversation and got to the honest core of it. Of course, now would be the perfect time to tell her that he and Georgina were no longer going to be married, that the big wedding catering job was not going to materialise, but he didn't. Instead he smiled lazily at her.

'If it stresses you out cooking for me, then of course I would not want you to feel obliged...'

'It doesn't *stress me out.*' She shuffled a few inches forward with her trolley.

'Good. Then no problem. Is it always this busy at a supermarket?'

Distracted, Francesca looked at him with an appalled expression. 'Angelo, could you keep your voice down when you make remarks like that? Of course supermarkets are busy places. When was the last time you set foot inside one?'

'Ah. Now let me think.' He began helping her take things out of the trolley, watching with amusement as she restructured his untidy piling up of items on the belt. 'I think I may have once gone into a very small one close to where I live.'

'And you don't want me to call you a dinosaur?' Francesca hissed. 'Look, please let me offload this trolley. Half the stuff you're cramming on is trying to fall off the sides.'

'Hence my argument for paying someone else to do the shopping for you.'

'Yes. If you have more money than sense.' And, of course, for most women, more money than sense in a man would be a very redeeming feature. He might be marrying Georgina because she fitted the bill, but how would he feel if perhaps she was marrying *him* because *he* fitted the bill?

'Or not enough time on your hands to wage World War Three in pursuit of a few items of food.'

'It's not always like this.' She grinned reluctantly at him. 'If you come at weird hours it's quite empty and you can fly around and get what you want without having to queue at the tills.' Walking at a snail's pace and insisting on looking at every jar and bottle didn't help either when it came to speed. She realised that they had been shopping for well over an hour. Time was ticking past. There was a meal to cook. The chances of him being out of her house by nine were beginning to look remote.

She was aware of him chatting to her, nothing that would put her on the defensive. Once or twice, as she was filling the bags while he stood next to her, under orders to let her handle the packing, he referred to their past. Little droplets of memories that warmed her inside. The bread shop they would go to in Venice. The patisseries in Paris, where they had occasionally stayed in her apartment when it had been more convenient with their overlapping schedules.

He insisted on taking the bags into the house. 'I'm more than competent when it comes to lifting heavy things,' he informed her seriously. 'Why don't you go and stick the wine in the fridge and put on some of that modern English music a dinosaur like myself has not heard of?'

There was no point arguing. She stuck the wine in the fridge, wondered what she was doing, put on some R&B music, wondered a bit more what she was doing, and then there he was, piling bags on to the kitchen table and hunting in the cupboards for a couple of glasses for the wine.

And still talking to her, as though they were the friends they no longer were.

'Let me help you,' Angelo said, pouring them both a glass of wine.

'What's the good of that if the point is to see whether I'm capable of producing good food?'

Angelo stifled the urge to inform her that producing good food, or food of any kind, was not the point of the evening for him. He also stifled the urge to tell her that she looked as sexy as hell kitted out in a black and white checked apron, that he would be interested in seeing how the apron looked without anything worn under it.

'I like the music,' he said, dropping his eyes and swirling his wineglass gently around. 'Sexy.'

The word dropped into the silence and rested there for a few moments. 'Where's Georgina this evening?'

'Paris, I believe.' Exhausting her rage through some retail therapy. Her mother would, no doubt, already have sympathised with her daughter that he was no good for her, a foreigner without any knowledge of how the British operated. The accusation had been one of the more choice ones from his ex-fiancée.

'You *believe*? That's a bit indifferent, Angelo. You should have asked her over here with you to sample my cooking.'

'I prefer to savour the revelation on my own.' He sipped some of his wine and caught her eyes over the rim of his glass.

The smoky intensity in his eyes went to her head like a bolt of lightning—a few heated seconds, plenty long enough for the sharply honed knife she had been wielding with such expertise to slice through skin.

With a little yelp, Francesca yanked her finger and dashed to the sink.

'Let me see it!' Angelo was next to her before she was even aware of him leaving the chair.

'It's nothing.' She gave him a wobbly smile. 'I don't normally chop my finger to bits when I'm slicing onions.'

'It's pouring blood. Where is your first aid box?'

'It's not pouring blood. It's…' The remainder of her sentence was lost in sheer shock as he raised her finger to his mouth and sucked it.

'Antiseptic,' he murmured as her body temperature rocketed upwards at an alarming rate. 'Did you know that? Let's go and find some plaster.'

'I have some in one of these drawers,' Francesca mumbled.

'Leave it to me.' He began pulling open drawers while

she stood, transfixed, staring, heart racing. He found the right drawer eventually and carefully began putting the plaster over the cut. His touch was electrifying.

'There's no need for you to do that, Angelo. I'm perfectly capable of putting on a piece of plaster myself.' Fat lot of good the protest was, she thought, when she was passively allowing him to do what he wanted.

'Nonsense. All women feel faint at the sight of blood. It's a well documented fact.' He looked at her and grinned. 'Fortunately I'm a man and therefore very good at dealing with situations like this.'

'That is the most…the most…'

'Truthful thing you have ever heard spoken?'

'The most *ridiculous* nonsense I've ever heard in my life.' The plaster was on but he was still standing right there in front of her, making it very difficult for her to breathe and impossible for her to move, with her back to the counter.

'You remember I once told you that for a while I toyed with the idea of studying medicine at university…'

'And *you* remember that I once replied that thinking about studying medicine didn't actually qualify you as a doctor?'

'I always thought that that was a particularly harsh response,' Angelo said piously, 'especially considering that I had just successfully diagnosed your stress-induced stomach ulcer as indigestion.'

For a few breathless seconds Francesca didn't say anything, then she muttered, looking away, 'I'll get on and do the cooking, then, if you don't mind. Thanks for putting on a piece of plaster for me and I don't mean to have the last word but I could have done it myself.' She turned away, waiting for him to return to his chair, which he did. She failed to hear his exasperated sigh. 'Actually,' she carried on, papering over her chaotic feelings with small talk, 'the catering course I went on was very good. We didn't just learn how to cook. We also learnt quite a bit about nutrition and how what we eat affects our health and well-being, and also some basic first aid measures for dealing with the sort of accidents that can happen in a kitchen. You know, cuts, burns, that sort of thing.' With her back to him, she could gather herself, get some kind of self-control going.

'Really. Interesting.' For a moment back then, he'd known that she was his, as dramatically turned on by him as he was by her. It hadn't lasted.

'Yes. Yes, it was. Very.' Prawns were cooked rapidly, dressing was made for the salad to accompany them.

'And was this the same course that your...boyfriend did?' Angelo drawled.

'Jack...no, Jack did another one, different place.'

Another brick wall. He decided to drop the subject. Damned if he was going to let her get away with an endless but safe conversation about the various methods of skinning tomatoes, though.

'You are making me feel guilty, sitting here, doing nothing.'

'You could always go for a walk and leave me here to get on with it,' Francesca suggested. 'I work better without an audience and you're right, it's boring for you just sitting down and watching.'

'I never said that I was bored. You're not drinking your wine.'

Francesca stopped what she was doing and took a long swig of the wine. Very expensive indeed. Light, crisp, dry with a nicely smoked flavour. 'There,' she said, looking at him. 'Satisfied?'

'Not quite yet,' Angelo murmured, finishing his wine and

rising to pour himself another. He would definitely have to get a taxi back to his apartment—if he needed to leave.

'Don't worry. The food won't disappoint but if you guzzle too much of that stuff you won't be able to appreciate it.' Back to the safety of the chicken and the olives and the frying. 'If you're bored, you can choose some different music to put on. My CDs are all in the rack behind you.'

Angelo could feel irritation starting to get the better of him. He swallowed it down and began looking through her collection of music, extracting random CDs, which he stockpiled on the kitchen table in a spreading, untidy heap.

Out of the corner of her eye, Francesca witnessed the encroachment of mess over the previously pristine surface and was not at all nonplussed. She had discovered early on in their relationship that, although Angelo was highly organized in his work life, in fact the most organised man she had ever come across, he was spectacularly untidy in his private life. Clothes were dropped and stepped over, ties were hung in gathering piles over any convenient surface, jackets were draped over backs of chairs with absolutely no thought to preserving their longevity. She had found it exasperating and curiously endearing at the same time.

'I hope you intend to put back all those CDs you've dumped on my kitchen table,' she said, covering the pan that held the chicken and taking time out to sit down with her glass of wine.

'Of course.' He paused in his frowning inspection of cases to shoot her a surprised look.

'Because your ability to be messy is legendary and I have no intention of clearing up behind you.'

Angelo frowned.

'And there's no need to look annoyed. I don't have to tiptoe around you.'

'When did you ever do that?' he demanded. 'I don't recall you ever doing that!'

'Oh. I forgot.' She drained her glass and stood up to fetch some plates from the cupboard. 'That was one of my faults. Lack of appropriate respect for the great Angelo Falcone!' Somewhere in her head she thought, *Oh, dear, shouldn't have said that,* but then why should she be on her agonisingly best behaviour? He was in *her* house, and not by her invitation. She would tell him that, should he want to pursue the conversation!

He didn't.

'Let us not argue,' he said mildly. He refilled her glass. 'Although, getting back to your accusation that I am a messy person, I challenge you to come to my apartment and test it for cleanliness.'

'Your housekeeper. Just like the one you employed in Venice. There's no point in arguing with evidence, Angelo.' She indicated the CDs on the table with a nod of her head and began laying the table, containing a sigh when he gathered up the cases and stacked them unevenly at the bottom of the table, meaning that he would sit far too close to her for her liking.

He shrugged and slipped on one of her classical CDs, beautiful, soothing music that rippled through the small kitchen like water trickling gently over stones. Soft, romantic music. Music to dance to in a flowing dress, in the arms of a lover. All wrong, she thought, for this particular situation. She had to keep reminding herself that the man was engaged, that he had treated her pretty badly, never mind his super-polite behaviour now.

She served the prawns while the chicken was still simmering and reddened with pleasure at the appreciative noises he made. When he poured her another glass of wine, she accepted.

'I hope you don't think that I drink this much when I'm preparing food for clients,' she said during a comfortable pause as she cleared away the prawns and began doing last-minute things to the main course. 'Because I don't.'

'Some of the finest meals are cooked while under the influence of good wine,' Angelo commented. 'That starter ranks up there.'

'You don't mean that.' With her back to him, she could feel her face glowing with pleasure. 'Do you?'

'Does it matter to you what I say?'

'Yes. You're a prospective client of mine. Of course it does!' Francesca could feel her voice rising, unnaturally bright. A bit like the colour spreading across her cheekbones. 'I'm always pleased when our food is complimented.'

Another brick wall. Three steps forward and two steps back, and every step back made the urgency inside him stronger. He didn't know what was driving him on to want this woman. He just knew that he did and if his reasons weren't exactly noble, then his awesome powers of reason were insufficient to steer him off course.

The one thing he did know was that this time it would be different for him. He would be utterly in control. He would get her out of his system and would be able to walk away from her without looking back.

But first he would have to break down the barriers between them. Swallowing back a sigh of frustration, he embarked on the least provocative line of conversation he could think of, asking her questions about the catering business generally, watching as she transferred food from saucepans and pots to basic white casserole dishes.

'Do you keep in touch with anyone from the modelling world?' he asked, when she had finally sat down and indicated to him that he should help himself.

Francesca laughed. 'Lord, no! I couldn't wait to get out of it in the end. For a start I was beginning to be the mother figure to a new crop of girls, all still in their teens. Some of them even had the adolescent spots to show for it!'

'I thought spots weren't allowed on models.' He didn't remind her that his offer for her to quit modelling, to move to London with him, had met with blank refusal.

'They're not. Hence the army of make-up artists who follow in the wake of every model. I've never met any spot that can't be successfully camouflaged under some expert face paint.' He was listening to every single word she was saying, giving her nonsense small talk his undivided attention. She had forgotten what a huge part of his charisma that was—the ability to listen.

'That used to irritate you, if I remember.'

Francesca's eyes skittered away from his dangerously good-looking face. 'I didn't miss it when I left. My face probably did, though!'

'You look better than you did then, if anything.' He willed her to actually look back at him and she did. 'Your hair suits you shorter. This chicken is very good, by the way. You do yourself a disservice when you say that Jack is the talent behind the cooking.'

'He thinks up unusual combinations. I know my limits. I stick to the things I know.'

'I don't believe you,' Angelo murmured. 'Only cowards stick to what they know. The predictable path is always the boring one.'

His voice was mesmerising. She tried to break the spell by eating, but, as always, the business of preparing the food had left her without any particular desire to sample it.

'I don't always stick to what I know,' Francesca retorted. 'But if the business is to succeed I can't just do exactly what I want, when I want!'

'And what would that be if you could?'

'What would what be?'

'What would you like to do if you weren't buttoned down chopping onions and preparing the same recipe over and over again because you've decided to leave the imaginative stuff to your boyfriend?'

'I am not *buttoned down*!' She jumped up from the table and began clearing up some of the used pans, her movements jerky. 'I might have known it wouldn't last!'

'What?' Angelo said tightly. He knew what. He had blown it. Just when he had actually got her to the point of dropping some of those damned defences, he had put her back up all over again. He should just drop this crazy idea, just realise that some challenges were a little too challenging.

'The politeness!' She folded her arms and glared at him.

'Oh, for God's sake!' He raked his fingers through his hair and glared right back at her. 'Being rooted in one place seems to have given you a keen sense of paranoia.'

'Paranoia?' She felt fired up with anger and safe within it.

'I'm not attacking you! I'm asking you if there are things that you still miss.'

You! The word shrieked in her head and she blanched. 'Like what?'

'Like travelling. Seeing the world.'

'I'm building a business. I haven't got the time or the finances to travel and see the world. Anyway, I did all that when I was younger.' She turned away abruptly and began filling the sink with soapy water for the dishes. She missed him. Yes, she had always known that, had always felt a little opening there in her heart, like a crack in the door just big enough to let a breeze laden with old memories blow through. What she hadn't realised until now was that the breeze was really a gale just waiting for the crack to get bigger.

'So now you've sampled my cooking, it's time you left.'

Maybe, just maybe, he would take the hint and actually do what she asked, so that without looking around she would simply hear the click of the front door closing and know that he had gone.

She wasn't aware of him approaching her until she was caged in by the sink, one strong, muscular bronzed arm on either side of her.

'You mean maybe it's time I left before I can say anything that you might not want to hear,' Angelo grated. 'And turn around and look at me when I'm talking to you!'

Francesca squeezed herself as far back as she could against the lip of the counter and manoeuvred herself round so that she was facing him.

'Don't you *dare* come into my house and tell me what to do! I want you to go now!'

'What else do you want me to do?'

'I have no idea what you're talking about!'

'Don't you?'

She knew he was going to kiss her. In that split instant the past and the present came crashing together as he lowered his head, raising one hand to curl into her hair. She thought that she might have whimpered a *no* but she couldn't push him away. Not when every nerve in her body was screaming for him to touch her.

His mouth collided with hers in a kiss that was scorchingly hot and hungry. God, it had been for ever and yet it felt like just yesterday. All that raging passion. She raised both her arms and wound them around his neck, pulling him against her, tasting him with the desperate urgency of a drought survivor tasting water.

Her eyes were closed when he finally pulled back, sucking in a deep breath of air. She followed suit, but reluctantly.

'The washing up can wait until later. Right now I want to continue this upstairs.'

Francesca nodded.

'That's not good enough. I want to hear you say it.'

'Take me upstairs, Angelo.'

It was all he needed to hear and it was music to his ears. With one swift movement he scooped her up, as though she weighed nothing, and headed out of the kitchen and up the stairs. Finding the bedroom was easy. There were only two and the door to hers was flung open, as though ready and waiting to invite them both in.

He barely took in the décor, the low bed with the uncompromising leather headboard, the long burgundy curtains that draped down to the floor, the series of photos on the walls which had been enlarged and framed, pictures of places she had been to in the past. He didn't even notice the one of Venice, a view which they had both enjoyed a million years ago.

He only noticed her. The way she looked at him as he deposited her on the bed, giving her time to change her mind and not knowing what the hell he would do if she did. Her eyes were hot and slumberous and they watched as he began stripping off his clothes. She probably didn't know it but it was the biggest turn-on he had had since…since.

He had slept with this woman before, had done the most intimate things with her, and yet he felt like a teenager all over again, getting undressed in front of a woman for the first time. Crazy.

The shirt hit the floor, followed by the belt, which he yanked out in one swift movement.

His hand hovered imperceptibly on the button of his trousers and Francesca couldn't help herself. She moaned. Very softly but not so softly that he didn't pick it up.

The trousers joined the shirt and belt on the floor and the state of his arousal was all too obvious against the fine cloth of his boxers. Right now he just wanted to rip her clothes off and plunge into her, satisfy this need that had taken him over and was killing him, but that, he knew, he couldn't do. Most of all, he wanted to pleasure her, very, very slowly.

A weak moonlight was filtering into the room, casting shadows across her body. He stood at the foot of the bed, naked, showing her how much he was turned on.

'Your turn now, my beauty,' he said huskily. 'I have been waiting for this…'

CHAPTER SIX

AFTER years of self-imposed sexual hibernation it was magical.

Every part of her body that he touched was suddenly brought to life. He stripped her very slowly and looked at her as if he was seeing her for the first time. He kissed her mouth, her face, her neck, trailed his tongue along her collar-bone and suckled on her nipples while she twisted hotly under him, fingers curled into his hair, her eyes closed as she drank up the sensations that were making nonsense of her common sense.

She felt the lean, hard lines of his muscular body and loved the familiarity and the newness of it.

When he paused to ask her whether she was protected, she nodded weakly. Well, one small lie never hurt anyone, did it? He hadn't come prepared with a condom and she hadn't used the contraceptive pill in years, not since they had split up. But her period hadn't long finished and she was safe.

Anyway, she couldn't have said no if she had tried. Her body was alive with need.

He thrust into her, sending her into orbit. Her little moans and whimpers became cries of ecstasy. It was just how it used to be. Just as shattering, just as glorious, just as fulfilling. More so, if anything, because she, too, discovered that she had been waiting for him.

Afterwards, lying on the bed next to him, reality finally began to kick in. Not in a rush, like you read in books, but in tiny little drops.

97

The clock on the dressing table was saying ten-thirty. Downstairs the main course of their meal, which he had intended to sample as proof that she was up to catering for his wedding, was still sitting around on plates and dishes. Francesca groaned and sat up, drawing her knees up to her chin and pulling the quilt up to her neck.

'And now you are about to tell me that this has all been a terrible mistake. Am I right?' He ran one finger along her spine, sending little shivers racing through her, and she turned around and looked at him. God, he was so beautiful. Unbearably beautiful.

'Of course it's been a mistake, Angelo.'

'Come back to bed.'

'Don't! How can you say that when…when…?' She stood up, feeling very self-conscious, and padded out to the bathroom where he could hear the sound of a bath being run.

Angelo did nothing to stop her. He knew her well enough to know that she would take her time with her bath, putting off the moment of having to return to the bedroom. He settled down, hands folded behind his head, to wait.

When she came in forty minutes later she was in fighting mood. She switched the light on immediately and stood by the door, hair washed and decently attired in some jogging bottoms that showed off more than a tempting amount of stomach and a loose, cropped jumper with deep pockets on either side and a hood. Her hands were thrust into the pockets as she stood there, glaring.

'I've had time to think, Angelo, and I've come to the conclusion that you're despicable.'

'Care to come a bit closer and tell me that?'

'No. What I *care* to do is remind you that you're in *my* house and that I want you to leave. And, if you're interested, I won't be doing the catering for your wedding so you'll have to find someone else.'

Angelo didn't budge. 'Turn off the top light. It's too bright in here.'

'Angelo. Go!' She strode into the room and snatched the quilt off the bed, revealing a highly tuned body in all its natural glory. If she had been hoping that he would lurch to cover himself with the nearest piece of fabric, she was mistaken. He remained where he was, looking at her with a lazy half smile, until she was forced to pick all his clothes up from the floor and throw them at him.

'I'm not about to put them on,' he commented, gathering them up in a pile and dumping them right back on the floor. 'If you want me to get dressed, then you're going to have to do it yourself. Which might very well be an interesting experience for the both of us.'

'This isn't a game,' Francesca shouted furiously.

'No. It is not. So why don't you stop behaving like a fishwife and tell me what it is that's bothering you? Has the quality of my lovemaking gone downhill? Hmm? Have I not satisfied you?' He knew what levers to pull to enrage her further but he wasn't going to rise to an argument. Not when he felt so pleasurably satisfied.

She had come to him, had been unable to resist. For a man who had once been victim to a loss of control when it came to her, he had felt superbly back in control, calling the shots.

'How could you come here...and *make a pass at me* when you're engaged to be married? And, to add insult to injury, I am the person who is supposed to be catering the wedding meal!'

This time Angelo sat up.

'And you are...what? Acting the outraged maiden doesn't impress me, Francesca. Have you conveniently forgotten that you have a boyfriend tucked away in the background?'

'Jack…Jack…'

'…wouldn't mind?' he inserted sarcastically. 'Isn't jealous? Believes in a strict policy of sharing, even when it comes to his women?'

Francesca sagged and walked across to the window, where she perched on the ledge and looked at him. It was very obvious where he was heading with his little argument. The 'pot calling the kettle black' argument. She had let herself go along with the fiction that she and Jack were involved because she wanted protection from herself. Now, to admit the truth would also be to explain the lie.

'You don't understand. And, anyway, we're not talking about me. We're talking about you and your seedy morals.'

'And yours are more noble?' Angelo laughed dryly. 'I wish you would explain how. I would be very interested to find out and if you can persuade me with your argument then I would advise you to drop the catering and go in for a career in law instead. There is always scope for a good barrister who can think creatively on his feet.'

'I hate you, Angelo Falcone.'

'No. You don't. If you hated me, you would never have climbed into bed with me. Especially considering you have a boyfriend. I know you well enough to know that much.'

'I don't…have a boyfriend.'

'Could you repeat that?'

'You heard me. I don't have a boyfriend. Jack and I aren't lovers and never have been.'

Angelo slung his legs over the side of the bed and looked at her thoughtfully as he scooped up the clothes from the floor.

'How interesting,' he drawled, walking towards her. 'Now, why would you lead me to believe that you were involved with someone else? Did you want to prove to me that you had moved on with your life?'

'Of course not! Would you mind getting dressed?'

'I'll do better than that. I shall go and have a shower and then, when I return, we can talk…' He strolled towards the door, pausing to say over his shoulder, 'Unless, of course, you want to keep me company in the shower?'

A cold shower. He needed it. Having tasted her, he realised that he wanted more. He emerged fifteen minutes later, fully dressed, to find her no longer in the bedroom but standing by the front door.

'If you think I am leaving, then you can think again,' he said, heading straight to the sitting room. 'Now that we have finally broken the ice, there is so much talking to do. Including,' he added softly, 'why you lied to me about Jack.'

Francesca reluctantly followed him to find that he had taken up position on the sofa, where he was reclining like lord and master, hands behind his head and his feet hooked over the low arm, giving him an eagle-eye view of her as she sat on the chair facing him.

The table lamp was still switched on and, for all the resentment seething through her, resentment at him for showing up and turning her world upside down and anger at herself for making love to him, she still found her eyes riveted by the startling reality of his physical presence.

He dominated the room. Just as he had dominated the kitchen. The whole house. Nothing new about that. He had always done that, captured the attention of everyone when he walked into a room. She used to tease him about it, feigning petulance because shouldn't she, as the model, be the one to rivet everyone? But she had enjoyed the feeling, loving the knowledge that, however many women followed his every move, he was hers.

Now, she just felt as though he was depriving her of oxygen.

'Well?' he prompted. 'Why did you lie to me?'

'Does it matter?' She looked at him with impotent hostility. 'I didn't lie when I told you that I loved him,' she said grudgingly. 'We just aren't involved with one another romantically and, actually, it wasn't my idea. It was Jack's.'

'Because…?'

'Because he thought that you might try and make a pass at me for old times' sake.' There was at least an element of truth there and it absolved her from any more in depth confessions, which was a blessing.

'And did *you* think that I might?'

'No. I *thought* you were a happily engaged man. I didn't realise then that you would be willing to cheat on your partner before you even took the marriage vows.' He deflected her neat turning of the tables with a careless shrug. 'But then again,' she continued, gaining some self-righteous momentum, 'I wasn't to know that your engagement was just a sham, that you weren't in love with your fiancée, just using her because she happened to have all the right connections and, of course, a man of your standing would have to have a woman with all the right connections. Silly me! Which brings us to Georgina. Are you going to tell her about me? About our past? About the fact that you came here and…and…'

'She will never know about our past. Why on earth should she?' Angelo said honestly. 'And I am glad you brought up my fiancée because I am curious to know how it is that someone so full of moral rectitude still ended up in bed with me. With a fiancée hovering in the background. You might have had your clear conscience when it came to Jack but did you not stop to consider the other person who might have been affected by our love-making?'

The silence stretched between them to breaking-point. She had laid down her own traps only to find herself neatly manoeuvred into a much bigger one, not of her making.

'No answer to that?' He stood up and flexed his muscles. 'We seem to have forgotten all about eating in the...urgency of things. No matter. You won't be catering now anyway.' The smile he gave her was the smile of a tiger watching the pointless antics of an antelope in full flight.

For a few seconds Francesca thought that he was moving over to where she was sitting, and for a few seconds Angelo considered it. Considered confronting her with the shaming truth that she had forgotten all about Georgina in her suffocating need to make love to him. He rejected the idea.

He also considered, for rather less time, the possibility of walking away from her now. For good. Wouldn't he be left with the pleasurable feeling of having finished business? Of having put a full stop at the end of the incomplete sentence? Once and for all?

Instead, he paused as he drew level with her and smiled. 'It's been a...revelation, seeing you tonight, Francesca. And I am very sure I will be seeing you again.' He looked at her and thought that he could make love to her again. Right now and right here, forget about the comfortable trappings of a bed.

'Over my dead body, Angelo. I might have made a mistake once but I learn quickly. I won't be making the same mistake again.' If only she could feel that. Deep in her bones where it mattered. Instead, she heard the heartfelt words roll off her tongue as she stared back up at him and was terrified that, put to the test, they would be as empty as a shell.

'I would love to stay and debate the definition of the

word *mistake*,' he murmured, 'but it's late. I should be getting back.'

The sound of the front door closing was, Francesca gloomily reckoned, roughly two hours too late.

She had emerged from the evening with her pride well and truly in tatters because her body had decided to break away and follow a course of its own. He had touched her and she had melted; it was as simple as that.

And off he had gone, back to Georgina and his well-ordered life. With, of course, another caterer to take over the joy-filled wedding celebrations.

She could have kicked herself. Could have kicked anything. And did. The chair. Followed by the door as she made her way upstairs, only to confront the shameful sight of bedclothes all tangled up, gleefully reminding her of her own lack of will-power.

It took half an hour to change the linen, another hour to put it in the washing machine and, once washed, into the tumble-drier. Hopefully it would eradicate the lingering aroma of lust but she knew that that was just paying lip service to a problem. In her head the lust was still there and, worse, it was all tangled up in emotions and feelings she didn't even want to start analysing too deeply.

It was after midnight when she reached for the phone and dialled Jack's number. The chances of interrupting his sleep were remote. On a weekend Jack made a point of getting as little sleep as possible and, sure enough, he answered his mobile in the slurred, happy voice of someone well past the point of sobriety.

'The catering job for the Falcone wedding is off,' she told him bluntly.

There was a long pause which she filled by getting a few things off her chest. The fact that it would have been impossible anyway, given the circumstances. The fact that she was well rid of her past, that confronting it and not walking away had been a mistake from the very beginning. Angelo Falcone, she declared vehemently, would probably never have chosen them on their merits. An unknown two-man band with zero experience of catering for huge amounts of people. He had chosen them because he had wanted to watch them both squirm in their inability to make the grade.

Jack sounded doubtful. 'I thought you said that he was going to give us a fair stab at it.'

'And he's obviously had a change of heart.'

'You mean he cancelled us? Just like that?'

'Sort of.'

'What does *sort of* mean?'

'It means that I was put in a position where there was no option but to back out. I'm sorry, Jack. We'll just have to build ourselves up slowly.' She had intended to pour her heart out, to tell him of her fiasco of an evening. After all, she and Jack shared everything. But at the last minute she had a change of heart. So at the end of fifteen minutes she hung up feeling as though, somehow, it had been a wasted phone call. Certainly not a call that warranted being made at midnight on a Saturday—one of the few Saturday nights they had taken off, so that Jack could watch his beloved cricket match. And she had got nothing off her chest. She went to bed with the same conflicting thoughts running rampant in her head and woke up, groggy and tired, in the same frame of mind.

The one salvation was that by the time Jack returned to London she was calmer, more able to explain why she had turned the job down after all, blaming it on her own insecurities, saying that she'd rather it went to an outside party than deal with the suspicion that she had only landed it because of a historical affair that had bitten the dust years ago. The guilt was too much, she explained, with a convincing display of sincerity. Yes, it would have been nice but…such was life. She left him to wonder what exactly had been the catalyst behind her sudden decision and opted for expressions of genuine regret at the passing of a great opportunity. Not, of course, overplaying her hand in case he decided to pursue the unfortunate situation of his own accord.

She also spent the next two days in a state of muted terror in case Angelo kept his promise and came back to call. She would never have expected it of him, would never have expected him to play around behind his fiancée's back, but maybe Jack was right, maybe men were all open to a bit of temptation. And she had not held back in her responses. Why not pursue the eager ex when the present fiancée was simply a business arrangement? Wouldn't that be how he might think?

She felt like a cat on a hot tin roof, jumping every time the telephone rang, every time someone came to the door with deliveries. She was expecting him to descend on her, and so, when she heard the doorbell of her own house trill at nine in the evening, hours after she had stopped work, she knew who it was going to be. Not Jack. She also knew that she was not going to take the chain off the latch.

She was rigid with tension as she opened the door a crack. She was also well rehearsed in exactly what she was going to say and the tone of voice she was going to use. Cold, distant, firm.

But it wasn't Angelo and her surprise took the wind out of her sails.

'Good evening, Mrs…uh…Miss…'

'Let me in. I want to talk to you.' Georgina's cut glass accent cut through her stammering like a knife through butter and Francesca found herself fumbling with the chain and pulling open the door.

She swept into the house in an elegant swirling cloud of yellow. Yellow jacket, yellow shoes, pale yellow clutch bag. She spent three seconds contemptuously taking in her surroundings before turning her full attention to Francesca.

Even though Georgina wore high heels Francesca towered over her, not that her height gave her any advantages. The only thought running through her head was that Angelo had told his fiancée about the lapse in his fidelity and Georgina, the business arrangement who wasn't jealous, obviously wasn't so much of a business arrangement that she hadn't seen fit to storm round and have her say. Her very furious say, judging from the expression on her face.

Francesca cleared her throat and tried to find a way out of the thick fog of guilt engulfing her.

'What…what can I do for you?'

'What can you do for me?'

'Look, I think I know why you've come here…'

'I'm sure you do,' Georgina said scathingly. 'I bet that bastard came running here just as soon as he could.'

Silence, Francesca thought, was the best form of self-defence. What she had done had been wrong. She deserved every bit of the attack about to be launched at her.

'I should never have considered you for the job. Never! I told Angelo that you were nothing but a two-bit company and I should have stuck to my guns. But oh, no! I thought I would be obliging and go along with giving you a fair try. Didn't know then what I know now, though, did I? And *you*, you…you *nobody*…didn't see fit to fill me in, did you?'

Francesca remained in mute silence, mortified and prepared to weather the onslaught. If she could have turned back the hands of time, oh, she would never have agreed to cook dinner for him, would never have agreed to let him into her house in the first place. If, if, if…

'Well, if you and Angelo think that he can break off the engagement so that the pair of you can walk into the sunset holding hands, while I'm left looking a complete idiot in front of my friends, then you're both in for a shock!' Georgina's porcelain skin was mottled with fury.

'He's broken off the engagement?' Francesca asked weakly. Oh, dear Lord. *Why?* She felt her legs on the verge of giving way and decided that sitting down might be a good idea. Crumpling to the floor in a heap would add to her mortification and, aside from that, those very pointed yellow shoes looked as though they could inflict severe damage when wielded by a tiny furious blonde.

'Perhaps we ought to sit down,' she said and left Georgina no option by heading straight into the sitting room.

'When…when did this happen?' she asked.

Georgina wasn't sitting down. She was pulsating by the window.

'Please don't pretend that you don't know. Five days ago.'

'*Five days ago?*' Francesca did the maths. So Angelo hadn't been playing around. He had come to her as a single man. Why hadn't he said anything? Maybe, she thought slowly, because he had come intending to seduce her and he figured his chances of success would have been lower had she seen herself as no more than a romp in the hay with a man who, even if he was the one to break off the engagement, would still be smarting from the sting of it.

Or maybe, she thought, digging into her knowledge of him, the way his mind worked, just maybe it had given him a kick to think that he could have her against all the odds, have her blinded to his situation by her own desires. And, if that was the case, had he really even *wanted* her? The way she had wanted him?

'How did you find out that Angelo and I...?'

'Had once been lovers? Well, certainly not from you! Nor from Angelo. Your partner, Jack, told me.' Her voice was laced with venom but Francesca still felt sorry for her, sorry for the marriage which wasn't going to take place, even if for Angelo it had only been a marriage of convenience. Even if it had only been a marriage of convenience for both of them.

'Jack...?'

'Although I would have twigged sooner or later. You might have tried to keep it under wraps but I would have found out. I would have made it my business to find out. Tell me, when did you decide that Angelo was a good bet? Did you see him and think that here was your chance to try and get him, having failed the first time? Or do you sleep with all your male clients in the hope that you might net one of them, and you had the advantage with Angelo because you had already been lovers?'

'I'm sorry about your engagement, Georgina, and I won't be walking off into any sunset holding hands with Angelo.' She stood up but didn't venture too close. Instead, she folded her arms and did her best to remember that, however guilty she felt, this was still her house and she could determine how much of the conversation she wanted to hear. Right now, no more of it. 'Now, I think it's time you left.'

'My pleasure. I just came to warn you that you'll never have him. I won't have him and neither will you. I'll see to it.'

'How?' Francesca asked coldly. Wrong question. Georgina obviously hadn't worked that one out yet. She delivered one last venomous look and turned on her heel. Not a backward glance. Francesca heard the front door slam and sagged in relief.

Then she hit the phone.

She'd expected to be furious with Jack, running to the viper blonde and blabbing things that were none of her business or anyone else's for that matter, but she wasn't. As he stammered out an explanation she could only sigh with resignation. He had been concerned about her, hadn't been able to bear her disappointment at losing the job, had just gone to see Georgina on the off chance that he could persuade her not to jettison the job because Francesca and Angelo had once had a fling years back. How was he to know that the engagement had already been called off? He had known halfway through the conversation that it had been a bad idea but by then it had been too difficult to back down and leave.

Francesca listened, letting him talk, until there was nothing left to say. She didn't see how she could tell him what had happened between her and Angelo. It just seemed too complicated and not very relevant anyway.

The reality was that they no longer had the job, for whatever reasons. It would have been nice, a juicy little add-on to their portfolio, but that, as they said, was life.

She wasn't angry with Jack.

She was, however, angry with Angelo. She had a few hours of restless sleep, during which her anger had time to grow, and by nine the following morning she was in no fit state to placidly start preparing desserts for the Hamiltons' supper party the following evening.

Along with the now redundant menus for the wedding that would never take place was his business card.

Francesca stuck on her most formal suit, a grey skirt with a snappy grey jacket, white shirt underneath, high heels that would elevate her almost to his height, and headed for the City.

She had left behind an uncomplaining Jack to cover her temporary absence. He was still smarting from his misjudged act of charity on her behalf and was only too happy to do what she wanted. He hadn't asked where she was going or why it was so important, nor did he quiz her on her flushed cheeks and over-bright eyes.

There never seemed to be a quiet time in the City, at least not during working hours, and today was no different. She took a taxi to his office.

What she had expected was precisely what she found. A tall smoked glass building housing branches of various financial institutions. Inside, the foyer was brightly lit. The broad marbled expanse would have been daunting had it not been for the clever interspersing of giant plants that looked as though they belonged in a jungle rather than in the bowels of a building in the centre of London.

Getting past reception was no problem. She gave Georgina's name, just in case Angelo had decided to ditch her after his ego-boosting coup at her expense. He might no longer be engaged to the blonde but he would never risk having her create a scene on his turf.

What a surprise, she fulminated on the way up in the lift, when he was confronted by a six-foot brunette instead of his ex-fiancée.

His business covered three floors of the impressive building and the directors' offices were on the top floor. The lift disgorged her into the hushed atmosphere of a library. People were busy with purpose—the purpose of making vast sums of money.

His secretary met her at the doors of the lift and said, with sweeping understatement, 'You're not Miss Thompson.'

'I need to see Angelo and I'm afraid I borrowed Miss Thompson's name to get up here.' His secretary had the sort of face that looked as though it responded well to honesty. 'I'm Francesca Hayley and I am…was…' Was the broken engagement public knowledge?

'The caterer. May I ask what your business here is, Miss Hayley?'

'Of a personal nature.'

There was a few seconds of silence, then the woman nodded. 'He has half an hour before his next meeting…I suppose I could let you see him…'

His office was at the very end of the elegant, expensive suite of offices. They passed thick wooden doors discreetly shut, behind which Francesca glimpsed the mechanisms of big business in operation.

Then they were at Angelo's door, which was open, although the connecting door that led directly to his office was shut.

'I would prefer to surprise him,' she murmured to the secretary, but that was taking good luck too far. She was shown in, although, when the door was quietly shut behind her, it was as good as a surprise because he was standing with his back to her, looking out of the window down to the matchstick people walking around outside.

'I cannot imagine what you want, Georgina,' he said, seemingly captivated by the view outside. 'I have said all there is to say.'

'Well, I haven't,' Francesca said. That brought a response. He spun around sharply. 'In fact, I've only just begun, Angelo.' She stepped forward. 'Why didn't you tell me that you had broken off your engagement with Georgina?'

'This is neither the time nor the place for a personal confrontation.'

'Conversation.'

'Whatever you want to call it.' He shrugged, looking at her, and used his intercom to tell his secretary to cancel his meetings for the morning. Taking time off work, something he never did, had never seemed so enticing. He had spent the past couple of days wondering what in hell he was doing. He had broken off his engagement, which he could see now had been a good thing, but still…would he have broken it off had it not been for the reappearance of Francesca in his life? Now he had slept with her and, like a man with an appetite not yet sated, he wanted more. But what for? He would never again make the mistake of offering her a relationship and he had already proved to himself that he could have her. Now she was standing in front of him like an avenging angel and his blood soared with wild elation.

'Did you plan on getting me into bed when you came round to my house?' Francesca asked bluntly, watching him as he grabbed his jacket.

'I told you. We'll discuss this out of my office.'

'Why? In case I throw a hissy fit and all your buddies come running to see what's going on?'

Angelo paused and looked at her. 'Now, why do you imagine that I would care what all my *buddies* think of me? You seem to forget that I own all of them. Who told you about the engagement?'

'Oh, I had a personal visit from your ex-fiancée. It seems she was a little less than impressed that you'd spent months leading her up the garden path only to cast her aside because, apparently, of me.'

Angelo shot her a cool smile. 'Georgina needs a reality check. How did she find out about you? I never mentioned it.'

'Jack.'

'Ah. The boyfriend that never was. Come on. We'll continue this somewhere else.'

'I don't want to continue this somewhere else.'

Angelo approached her, his face a grim, unsmiling mask. 'Let's get one thing straight, Francesca. You are not throwing a tantrum in my office. You will either leave with me now, and be grateful for the fact that I am making a space in my very packed diary to accommodate you and whatever gripes you seem to have, or you will leave.'

She sighed heavily and acquiesced, maintaining a steady silence until they were out of the building.

'Where are we going?'

'Somewhere more private than an office block.' He hailed a taxi, leaned in to the window to give the driver an address, while Francesca scrambled into a seat and waited, bristling, for him to join her.

She opened her mouth to talk and his mobile rang. While she continued to bristle he spoke into his phone, not looking at her. A long, detailed conversation to do with work. She might as well have been invisible.

Loosely translated, his behaviour was spelling out what she had already suspected. Angelo had made love to her, but not because he cared about her. Years ago he had cared about her, truly cared. Now he just wanted her. She also had to face the cruel fact that her anger was all about the stark truth that she had made love to him and her heart had opened out and welcomed him in, had been waiting in some foolish way for him to return.

He finished the phone call at roughly the same time as the taxi pulled up in front of an elegant Georgian house set in a crescent of identical houses—gleaming, beautifully proportioned white façades, black wrought iron railings and, lining the pavement outside, sleek, fast cars.

'Where are we?'

'My place. You want to talk? We'll talk in total privacy.' And those cool, dark eyes on her, melting her in places she didn't want, stirring up all kinds of things she could do without, because of the sickening realisation that whatever he had once felt for her had been stripped back to the barest bones, leaving only a searing passion that would never destroy him but very well might destroy her.

CHAPTER SEVEN

His house was larger inside than it appeared on the outside. Three floors, each of them compactly and efficiently laid out. The front door opened into a hall with sepia-coloured marble tiles, from which she glimpsed a door leading to a small sitting room. She followed him away from that towards the kitchen which dipped down three stairs and which was a functional blend of chrome and wood.

He made straight for the coffee percolator and began brewing some coffee while Francesca maintained a fuming presence at the door.

'Sit down,' he said, without bothering to turn around and look at her. 'You know you will eventually, anyway.'

'Why didn't you tell me that you had broken off your engagement with Georgina when you came around to my house?'

Angelo turned round slowly and looked at her, arms folded. 'Because I wanted you to make love with me thinking that I was still engaged. I wanted you to be so blinded by desire that your well-structured sense of morality would not have been able to overcome your physical craving.'

'You…you…' Francesca looked at him and struggled to find the right words to convey the depth of her disgust.

'Arrogant bastard?' he interjected helpfully.

'How *could* you?'

'Oh, don't think that it was passionless curiosity on my part. It wasn't. I wanted you every bit as much as you wanted me.'

'But you had a bruised ego to take into account and what

116

better way to apply some balm to it than by proving to yourself that you still had sufficient power over me to have me against the odds?'

'Something like that.' He shrugged and returned to the business of making them some coffee, some very strong coffee. She looked as though she could do with it and, frankly, he couldn't blame her. He had reduced their night of passion to a game with a winner and a loser. His bruised ego, as she had put it, should have been feeling considerably less bruised, bearing in mind that he had been the winner in the game, but it wasn't. Not that he was about to share this with her. No, he had learnt that emotional revelations were the first steps to vulnerability and vulnerable was not a place he intended to occupy again.

He handed her the cup of coffee, noting how her hand shook as she took it.

'I never thought…' Francesca managed to make it unsteadily to one of the kitchen chairs and sank into it. 'I never thought that you could…use me like that, Angelo.' Of course she did! The minute she had learnt of the broken engagement, of the timing of it, she had known in her heart that he had used her. It was her own fault that she felt sickened by the fact. Was she now going to give him the further satisfaction of seeing her break down in front of him, all her emotions displayed like lines on a page waiting to be read? She realised how much her hands were shaking, enough to make her spill the coffee if she wasn't careful. She sat on them and took a few steadying breaths, not looking at him, although she knew that he was looking at her, coolly and dispassionately.

'I'm not the man you used to know,' Angelo commented neutrally. 'Nor are you the same woman I used to know.'

'Why did you break off your engagement?' This time she did look at him and was proud that she met his unwavering gaze steadily. In fact, he was the first to break eye contact, pushing himself away from the counter and moving to straddle one of the chairs facing her.

'It wasn't fair on her,' he said. 'On either of us. A business arrangement is fine but it depends on both partners playing by the rules.'

'And your rules didn't include emotions.'

'I also discovered that what passed for sexual attraction to Georgina wasn't quite as…satisfactory as it could have been…' This time she was the one to look away as his stare became unbearable to hold.

'Well, now that you've explained things to me, I think I'll leave.' Her legs felt much steadier now. She felt that she might actually be able to balance herself on them.

It had been a good decision to confront him. He had been truthful with her and, sure, the truth was hurting her all over, even in places that were too deep to access, but at least there were no unanswered questions in her head. She remembered the way she had left him—had left him with swarms of unanswered questions—and flinched with guilt.

'Already? Don't you want to hear what else I have to say?'

No, because I know it'll hurt. But then walking away from him for ever would hurt too. What harm in delaying the inevitable by just a few more minutes? She sat back down and attempted to drink some of the coffee.

'What else could there be to say, Angelo? You can congratulate yourself on taking away my pride. Now the scores are finally even.'

Angelo flushed darkly, not liking the way that sounded, but knowing that she had every right to level the accusation.

'Poor Georgina. No wonder she came storming into my house. You took away hers as well, Angelo. Does that make you feel good?'

'No. No, it doesn't,' he said grimly. 'Her consolation is that she is well rid of me. She would have had a miserable marriage.'

'Big of you. I'm sure she's feeling very *consoled* already when she thinks about that.'

'Dammit, Francesca!' He ran his hands through his hair and stood up abruptly, pushing the chair back.

'I know. Horrible, isn't it? Having a woman answer you back. I may have changed in three years, Angelo, but I haven't changed that much. I still speak my mind. Oh, I forgot, that's one of the reasons I was so unsuitable.'

'But one of the reasons why you fire me up.' He came to stand by her and leaned down so that his face was inches away from hers. 'Georgina never fired me up.'

'And I'm supposed to feel flattered by that?' She felt her pulses quicken as she breathed him in, that unique, male scent with just the merest hint of aftershave that sent her senses soaring. She gulped and wished that she had left when she had the chance. Now she would have to push him out of the way to get past and she didn't want to touch him, didn't trust herself.

'Just like I feel flattered that you slept with me even when you thought that I was engaged to another woman. So you see, the scores are even.'

'Don't do that.'

'What?'

'Twist things around.'

'Is that what I'm doing? Or am I only being utterly truthful? I wanted you, Francesca, even when I was engaged to be married. Against all odds. That's saying something, isn't it?'

'What is it saying, Angelo?' Her breath caught in her throat at the expression in his eyes as they darkened.

'That we're still attracted to one another after all this

time and despite all the water that's flowed under the bridge.' He straightened up, giving himself time to get his act together and his raging body time to cool down. 'Let's finish this in the sitting room. Kitchen chairs are too uncomfortable for a full and frank discussion about how much we still want each other.'

Francesca stood up and heard herself mumble a weak refusal which he ignored, taking her hand instead and leading her out of the kitchen and into the sitting room.

It seemed the most natural thing in the world for her fingers to be entwined in his. Years ago, they used to walk like this, hand in hand, enjoying everything life had to offer. But this was now and it amazed her to find that it still felt good to be holding his hand, even though so much bad feeling stood between them. It hardly seemed possible but here she was, allowing herself to be led towards the sitting room. Away from the front door.

Sunshine poured into the sitting room and Angelo went to the windows and half closed the wooden shutters, immediately reducing the bright light to subdued strips that accentuated the deep, warm colours in the room.

Francesca had moved to the sofa and he joined her there. His fingers still tingled from where hers had been touching them. Crazy, the sexual chemistry that still existed between them.

'I meant what I said about…both of us having changed and I have a proposition for you.' He leaned forward, arms resting lightly on his thighs, and linked his fingers together.

'What kind of proposition?'

'The kind that acknowledges what we have and what we can't fight against.' His voice was calm, cool and controlled. Francesca fought to follow suit. 'An arrangement of sorts,' he said conversationally. 'One of a passionate nature. Passion with no strings attached. I never expected us to run into each other again and I certainly never expected that I would still be attracted to you, but we did and I am and you feel the same way.'

'You don't know what I feel, Angelo.'

'Oh, but I do.' He relaxed back and crossed his legs. Sexy, elegant and composed. 'Actions speak so much louder than words.'

'What would be the point?' Suddenly she couldn't sit still any longer. Nor could she withstand the shuttered steadiness of his gaze. She walked jerkily across to the bay window and perched on the ledge, wrapping her arms around her. How could he sit there and discuss them sleeping together as nonchalantly as if he was discussing the weather? 'You would want it to lead somewhere, wouldn't you? Isn't that what you said all those years ago?'

'What happened years ago is an irrelevance. It's what's happening now that matters. We want each other. Sufficient for me to break off my engagement, sufficient for you to sleep with me when your head was telling you not to.' He shrugged. 'I'm looking for nothing from you and you want nothing from me. Beyond the obvious.'

'It's crazy.'

'Come and sit back down.'

'What difference will that make?'

'Come and sit back down.'

She would have made for one of the chairs but that would have looked cowardly, so she stuck her chin up and sat next to him, face averted.

'Look at me. Unless, of course, you're too scared to do that.'

'Scared? Why should I be scared?' She faced him with a glare and sank straight into the fathomless depths of his black eyes. It really was a drowning sensation.

'Feel it?' he murmured, making no move to get closer to her, just watching her.

'No! Feel what?'

'That undercurrent that runs between us. It's irresistible, Francesca. That's why I think we should continue seeing one another, sleeping with one another, and this time we'll both know the boundaries and won't overstep them.'

'And if I say no? Which,' she added hurriedly, 'I will.'

'Then you leave. It's as simple as that. You know where the front door is. But I hope you don't.' He reached out and lazily coiled one finger into her hair, twining it round into a spiral before letting it drop.

But I hope you don't. She knew what she ought to do. Faced with a pool of quicksand yawning by her feet, she just had to turn around and walk away across solid land to safety. Nothing could ever come of anything between them.

But for just a little while she could have some stolen happiness. The past three years had been a wasteland. She had thrown everything into her career and enjoyed it, but the emotional side of her that had needed tending had been allowed to grow into a wilderness through lack of care.

'What you're proposing is…preposterous, *primitive*…'

'I'm a primitive man but never preposterous. What I am proposing is a solution.'

He stroked his finger along her collar-bone and Francesca sighed.

'And how long until this solution becomes redundant?' she asked quietly.

'Who knows? How long is a piece of string? All we know is that we will be able to satisfy our hunger for one another and then we will move on to find our proper destinies.'

'I can't believe I'm actually sitting here having this conversation with you, Angelo.' She eyed the door. 'I thought you were just making time to hear my gripes. Don't you have important meetings to rush off to?'

'Oh, nothing that I can't put on hold if I need to. Consider the day yours if you're brave enough to take the plunge.'

She stood up and he hooked his fingers around her wrist and with a little tug pulled her back down, in a tangle on his lap, laughing as she stared up at him with affronted eyes, laughing and sure of himself, of her.

She was clear-headed only for the length of time that it took for his mouth to find hers and, when it did, she sank into the kiss like a drowning man finding land. She felt the thrust of his tongue against hers and groaned when his hands curved beneath the formal white shirt, pushing it up until he was cupping her breast, feeling its weight through the lacy bra.

Then he was sliding down on the sofa, taking her with him and fumbling with the small buttons of her blouse. Now the shirt was finally off. Getting his own off was considerably quicker, especially as he didn't give a hoot if he ripped a few buttons off in the process. He just wanted her naked and on top of him.

Although there was a lot to be said for watching her luscious breasts in that sexy, low-cut lacy bra. As if reading his mind, or maybe reading his mind was just something she could do, she raised herself up, dangling her breasts over him and smiling when, with a little growl of impatience, he scooped them out of their constraints so that he could lower one pouting nipple into his mouth.

'Kinda sexy making love to a semi-clothed business woman,' he murmured roughly and Francesca made a noise halfway between a laugh and a moan as his mouth continued to circle her tightened bud.

He sucked on the moistened circle, pulling it deep into

his mouth, and ran his hands along her thighs and up her skirt until he could loop his fingers over the elasticated waist of her underwear, which he proceeded to pull down, allowing her to squirm her way out of them completely.

He was bare-backed but still in his work trousers and he could feel his throbbing erection pushing against the zip. Anticipation soared through him. He pulled down the zip of her neat grey skirt and watched as she stood up and completed the job of divesting herself of the last piece of clothing covering her.

'Shall we go upstairs?' Francesca glanced back towards the door, then looked at Angelo, comfortably sprawled on the sofa, his eyes fastened on her.

He had been right. *They* had been right. Right to acknowledge the power of their mutual sexual attraction, right to eliminate all the frills and fuss of possible emotional ties that would never happen. He wanted her, she wanted him, and his invitation was to indulge their joint desires until such time as they presumably became bored with one another. Of course, he would be the one to grow bored with her. That was just a reality she would have to accept and deal with because without any emotional ties whatsoever boredom followed hard on the heels of predictability and her initial allure would soon become tarnished around the edges. She would deal with that when the time came. She, too, would indulge her desires and her love which could never amount to anything, not with a man like him. It would be better than nothing—which, frankly, was what she had had for the past three long years.

'This sofa is big enough for the both of us,' Angelo said thickly, devouring her naked body with his eyes and restraining himself from leaping up and dragging her down to the ground like an animal on heat. 'Unless advancing middle age has made you lose that exploring edge of yours.'

Francesca laughed, picked up the nearest cushion from one of the chairs and threw it at him. 'Middle age indeed! I'm twenty-seven!'. She approached him, knelt down by the side of the sofa and cupped his beautiful face in her hands, sighing as he stroked her back. 'You should be the one to be careful, Angelo. You're an old man compared to me. No need to prove your virility by pretending that you're still capable of making love in unusual places.' She giggled and kissed him on the mouth, stifling his immediate protest. With one hand, she slowly fiddled with his belt, finally unhooking it and setting to work on the button of his trousers and the zip. She could feel the hard bulge that told her how much he wanted her and was fired by a wild, giddy passion.

'Prove my virility? You realise that you've laid down a gauntlet and, like any self-respecting red-blooded male, I'm going to have to take it up?'

. He did. On the sofa and, later on, in his massive king-sized bed. It was only when the sunlight began to mellow behind the gauze curtains that Francesca glanced at her watch and let out a little yelp.

'It's after five!'

'So what?' *So what?* He had missed a string of appointments. A first for him. His mobile phone had probably been going mad in the pocket of his jacket downstairs. He didn't care. For the first time in weeks he felt liberated and in control. He had acknowledged his feelings, acknowledged that the woman lying next to him, rather making a show of getting up, was the woman who still turned him on. He had wanted her and not simply to even scores or salve the ego that had been blasted to hell three years previously. He had just wanted her.

And now he could have her. He was a free man and he could have her without any uninvited feelings getting in the way of his enjoyment. He had told her just how it was, had left it up to her to decide whether she wanted to have a relationship with a man whose only feelings towards her were ones of lust and desire, had been more than prepared to shrug and walk away if she had turned him down. No questions asked, no blinding rages, no backward glance. Those times were long gone. He was a man utterly in control and it brought a smile of satisfaction to his lips.

'Where are you going?' he asked lazily, dragging her back down on to the bed and propping himself up on one elbow to stare at her.

'The day's practically gone, Angelo! I had no idea how long we'd spent… I had stuff to do…'

'So did I,' Angelo pointed out. He feathered a kiss on her mouth and his satisfaction went up a couple of notches as she helplessly responded. Really, she should have stormed out on him the minute he told her that he had deliberately kept her in the dark about the broken engagement for no better reason than he had wanted to see just how much she wanted him. She should even now be at home, breathing fire at his arrogance. But here she was, proof that she wanted him just as much as he wanted her. The past had blinded him to what was really a very simple truth, which was that had he still had any feelings for her he would never have forgiven her and had her back. That would have been weak and sad and he was neither weak nor sad. No, his only weakness was sex and that was entirely acceptable. He felt deliriously happy in a way he had not felt for a very long time, not even when he had been engaged to Georgina and heading down a path that had seemed entirely sensible and fitting.

Francesca groaned. 'Your meetings! Wouldn't your secretary have called? To remind you?'

'She probably did, on my cellphone, which is conveniently located out of hearing. She wouldn't have got through on this number. It's ex-directory and barred to everyone but a handful of close friends and relatives. This is the one place where I don't allow work to intrude if I don't want it to.'

'I never realised there was such a place,' Francesca said dryly. 'Anyway, I've got to go. I have things to buy and if I don't hurry I won't get to the shops in time.'

'What things?' He ran his hand along her thigh and felt her suppressed sigh. 'A few olives and some tomatoes? It can wait until tomorrow.'

'I have to get back and start doing what I should have been doing today. Lord, Jack must be wondering what's happened to me!'

'Let him wonder. Today we celebrate.'

'What exactly are we celebrating?'

'What do you think?' He raised his eyebrows and treated her to an expression very much like the one worn by the cat that had got the cream. 'We make great lovers and here we are, doing what we should have been doing all along.'

Francesca tried not to think too far ahead. Pondering on the destination of a road leading nowhere wasn't exactly going to put her in the perfect frame of mind and, having told herself that she would enjoy the present and not live beyond it, even in her darkest thoughts, she wanted to maintain her perfect frame of mind. And, yes, it *did* feel perfect. Right here, wrapped up with this man, the sunlight fighting a losing battle against the thickly bunched gauze curtains, the day lost in a haze of blissful love-making.

'I'm a little hungry.'

'That's a very pedestrian way to greet my remark,'

Angelo complained, thinking how much he had missed her forthrightness. 'Shall we go out for dinner? I know a very nice little restaurant just around the corner...'

'You mean get dressed, walk somewhere, order food, wait for food, eat it, then drag the remainder of the evening out with coffee? That sounds a little long.' She grinned and nudged her leg along his. His body felt slick, as hers did, from the physical exertion of making love. 'I could rustle up something from your fridge.'

'I'm not sure that's such a good idea,' Angelo drawled.

'Why not?' Francesca was genuinely puzzled. Once upon a time they had cooked together, or rather she had watched him while he cooked, lounging around in one of his shirts, in that little apartment in Venice. Now that she herself had become a cook, and one in demand, it made no sense to her that they should hunt out cuisine in any restaurants.

'Because what we have now,' he told her dispassionately, 'is all about sex. It's not about domesticity and cooking.' Never again would he go down that road with this particular woman. He could look back now at the past and in retrospect make a couple of very good deductions as to how she had managed to insinuate herself beneath his skin to the point where he had recklessly allowed himself to become vulnerable. It had been an easy enough road but a slippery one. The sex had turned into something warmer and more comfortable, and lazy, snatched evenings in his kitchen with the sound of some classical music wafting in the background while they played at being real partners had been the first step downhill.

'Oh, right. Yes. I understand.'

'I hope you do, Francesca, because if you don't then we might just as well call it off right now.'

He was deadly serious.

'It would be a shame, considering how much pleasure we give to one another, but it would be life...'

The rush of hurt that followed his words, his casual indifference to anything intimate between them aside from intimacy of a purely physical nature, was intense. Why the hell should she be hurt? It wasn't, she reminded herself, as though she could ever, *ever* allow her relationship with Angelo Falcone to go anywhere. What he had offered was just what suited her, the only thing that *could* suit her, when it came to him. It was lunacy to get wistful about something as trivial as sharing the cooking.

'Are you sure it's okay for us to even *be* here?' she asked ingenuously. 'In your townhouse? Considering it's all about sex, wouldn't it make more sense for us to meet in a hotel somewhere? Maybe we should think about eliminating conversation completely.'

'Now you're being ludicrous.'

'If a No Cooking rule applies on the premises, then that's fine with me.' She hated herself for the desperation that kept her rooted to the spot, but if he was using her then wasn't she similarly using him? She loved him and wanted him and if she chose to indulge those feelings for a while, then what was wrong with that?

For the first time, she envied Jack his cavalier attitude towards members of the opposite sex, the blithe manner in which he could have passing relationships and be perfectly happy. It was a damn sight healthier than being hunkered down in a hole of her own making.

'Just so long as you know that you'll never sample my fabulous cuisine now, even if you begged.' She kept her voice light as she slipped out of the bed and headed towards the *en suite* bathroom.

Angelo followed her. He had had to be frank with her but, still, it was a relief that she hadn't walked out. Not that it would have been the end of the world, but it would have been a tad disappointing when his expectations had been raised.

She wasn't aware of him pushing the door open and for a few seconds he stood there and stared as she stepped under the shower, catching her hair in her hands and raising her face to the shower head. She had the most exquisitely graceful body he had ever seen.

He entered the shower cubicle before she was even aware that he was in the bathroom and relieved her of the shampoo.

'Stay still,' he ordered, massaging it into her hair. With her back to him, his imagination provided all the necessary details of her nudity, turning him on even as his fingers worked their magic on her scalp. He rinsed her hair, then took the soap and very thoroughly began soaping her, sliding his hands along her shoulders and then over her breasts.

'I don't want to do a rushed job of this,' he murmured into her ear, as she arched back against him, 'so you'll have to keep as still as possible.'

Francesca allowed the luxurious sensuality of the moment wash over her, just like the warm darts of the shower were washing over her body. When he was touching her like this there was no room in her head for thought and that was fine because thinking wasn't something she wanted to do. It was something she couldn't afford to do. She gasped as his fingers played with her nipples before travelling down across her belly, then between her legs, which she parted as his fingers probed places that made her want to squirm.

'You're moving,' he warned.

'And you're impossible.' She spun around, laughing, dripping, wanting him so much that it hurt. Her body felt alive and fired up and, without bothering to switch off the shower, he took her. She barely noticed the discomfort of the marble wall against her back as he thrust into her and they came together, a powerful explosion that had him panting and propping himself up, eyes shut, his body shuddering from the aftermath of his orgasm.

The last thing Francesca felt she needed was the bother of getting dressed and setting foot outside the heated cocoon they had created for themselves, but dress she did, blow-drying her hair until it gleamed. The only make-up she had was in her bag, and amounted to no more than some mascara and lipstick, but when she looked back at her reflection it was glowing. A woman in love and living dangerously. Not a good combination.

She caught him looking at her in the mirror and smiled, asked him about the restaurant, teased him that too much rich food would have him putting on weight and enjoyed the sound of him laughing back with her. Keeping it light all the time.

They strolled to the restaurant, which turned out to be an Italian and a very good one.

Looking at her across the table, he was amazed to find himself getting turned on by her, by the habit she had of resting her chin in her hand and frowning slightly, as though every piece of conversation was being given the utmost consideration. Even when the topic of conversation happened to be work, a subject guaranteed to turn off the most ardent female and therefore one he had never felt the slightest inclination to discuss. Francesca, though, made a good listener. She offered opinions, which, he had to admit, were not entirely frivolous, and teased him out of his seriousness by telling him one or two amusing anecdotes about her own job and the near disasters they had had over the years.

Nearly two and a half hours later, Angelo was prepared

to admit that he felt relaxed. Relaxation, he reasoned, was not an intrusion into the ground rules he had laid down. Sex was one thing, but it had to be interspersed with something else. Obviously, not as a rule, but occasionally they might surface sufficiently to go out for a meal and at such times conversation was fine.

Perfectly satisfied with how the day had progressed—in fact, how *life* seemed to be progressing at the moment—he instinctively began walking back to his townhouse. Lord knew, but the blood was already surging through his veins at the prospect of ravishing her again. After a couple of steps he realised that she wasn't next to him. In fact, spinning round on his heel, he saw that she was standing on the kerb, hand outstretched to hail a passing cab.

'What are you doing?' he demanded, waving away the taxi that had slowed down for the fare.

'Going home.' Francesca looked at his darkly scowling face and smiled. 'It's late and I'm going to have to get up early to catch up on all the things I should have done today but didn't get around to.'

Angelo looked at her through narrowed eyes, weighing up whether to try and entice her back to his house. He knew he could. Instead, he nodded and smiled. All told, it wouldn't be a good idea to have her back anyway. It was late and he had no intention of her sleeping over.

'I'll call.'

Francesca dropped her eyes. Those two words said it all. She had become the puppet and he the all-powerful puppet master, holding the strings, in control. If sweet revenge had been what he was after, then he had got it because he had reduced her to a state of voluntary helplessness. But she believed what he had told her, that revenge was not the name of the game. If it had been, he would have walked away the very first time he had proved to himself that he could have her. He certainly would not have broken off his engagement with Georgina and wrecked his perfect plans. Angelo Falcone was not a man to disturb the onward march of his well-planned life on the spur of the moment. He wanted her and had given her the option of satisfying him and herself in the bargain, and she had taken it because she was a coward when it came to him. He had stormed back into her life and revealed it for what it was. A life devoid of any emotional passion or connection to anyone else, given meaning only by virtue of the career she had chosen.

She nodded and turned away, stretching out her hand once again for a passing cab. She neither expected, nor was surprised by the fact that he didn't see fit to wait by her side until one arrived. Why should he? She meant no more to him than a body that could excite him. Any feelings beyond that were illusory. They could chat and laugh but her main purpose was to be his willing bed companion. Everything else orbited around that one central need.

And she would do it, because she loved him and loved life when he was in it, for better or for worse.

The fact that her circumstances would never change, that she would never be able to even dream of anything more, was her cross to bear.

In the meantime, she would snatch what she could get. A black cab pulled up and she hopped in, tempted to look back and seek him out, and making herself stare straight ahead, destination unknown.

CHAPTER EIGHT

Something wasn't quite right. Angelo could feel it in the small breaks in conversation, during which her eyes slid away from his and her hand fiddled with the damn wineglass, from which she was drinking very little.

'Okay, you might as well spit it out. What's wrong?' The Italian restaurant, at which they had dined for the first time almost six weeks ago, had become their staple eating out place. It was convenient and convenience counted when sitting down and eating was something that they wanted to do in the minimum amount of time.

Because their need for one another had not diminished. Angelo looked at her broodingly across the table and raised his wineglass to his lips. He was mildly surprised that she was still a fixture in his life, considering they now saw each other several times a week, which had given him ample time to grow bored, but he wasn't questioning the situation. He just knew that when he clicked his fingers she came running and that suited him superbly. He had also been careful not to allow any complacency to enter into the well-oiled arrangement. No cosy cooking in the kitchen, not even a take-away. They either ate out or didn't bother to eat at all. And no sleeping over. He left, whatever the time, when they utilised her house and she did the same when, as more often than not, she came to him. His boundaries were perfectly intact, allowing him to enjoy himself without any bothersome stirrings of conscience or doubt.

'Nothing.' Francesca dragged her eyes back to him and forced herself to smile. 'I'm not very hungry.'

'So I notice. But I'm not buying that as an excuse. So tell me what's wrong. Some catering job not going according to plan? Or are you worrying about Jack again? He's a big boy. He can take care of himself.' He had heard a great deal about Jack over the past few weeks, entertaining stories of his various escapades, some of which left her tearing her hair out in despair.

'I know that,' Francesca said, staring down at her plate and contemplating the arrangement of chicken and sautéed potatoes there which was making her feel slightly nauseous.

'So what then?'

She detected the hint of impatience in his voice and winced. Mood swings were not part of the deal.

'What if I told you that I was tired? That I just wasn't in the mood to go back to your house tonight and make love? Or that yes, I wanted to go back to your house, but to talk.'

'Talk about what?'

'Anything.' Francesca shrugged. 'What you've been up to. What I've been up to. The weather. The crisis in the Health Service. Why it always seems to rain on weekends. *Anything.*'

'We know what each other has been up to. The weather is autumnal. The Health Service always seems to be in a mess, and it rains on weekends because the English climate is unpredictable, diabolical and likes to see people cancel their planned activities at the last minute. There, covered.' He signalled for the bill and continued watching her while he waited.

'So it is. I'm glad we got that out of the way. Now we can repair back to your place and do what we do best.'

'Long evenings spent chatting isn't what this is about, Francesca. I thought you understood that.' He saw the way she flinched and was tempted to exercise a bit more compassion, but he resisted. No point in setting precedents that he would then find himself compelled to continue fulfilling. He wasn't in the business of building a relationship with her. He had been there, done that and had the tee shirt to show for his efforts. Besides, he thought, they talked, didn't they? How much more conversation was she looking for?

'I do understand, Angelo. I don't know what came over me.' Now she was beginning to feel emotional, saying all sorts of stuff that she hadn't intended. She certainly hadn't intended to launch into a tirade about wanting to go back to his place and bond on some kind of spiritual, platonic level. The opposite. She had been looking forward to seeing him, to sleeping with him before she broke her news. She hadn't planned on an emotional outburst which would leave him cold and withdrawn.

Angelo, expert as he was at second-guessing other people, recognised her wobbly smile for what it was, a plaster covering up something else, and for a fleeting second felt a chill of foreboding sweep through him before he reminded himself that there couldn't possibly be anything substantially wrong. He had seen her two days ago and they had spent an amazing four hours together, a marathon and lazily indolent evening during which they had not managed to struggle out of his much-used king-sized bed. And, dammit, they had talked then, hadn't they? What could have happened in the space of two days to have brought about this sudden and unwelcome shift in atmosphere?

Had Jack been talking to her? He knew that they shared some kind of bond, although the reasons behind it were beyond him, but that being the case, maybe the man had put notions in her head, notions about the wisdom of getting involved in a purely sexual relationship that wasn't going anywhere. From what she had told him, Jack was the last person to lecture anyone on the importance of building relationships but then people who lived in glass houses were often the ones who threw the most stones. And, like it or not, she paid heed to things the man said, which was something he found irksome but was willing to put up with in view of the fact that they were just friends. He did not feel inclined to be quite so generous if the man had been putting ideas into her head. In fact, he would have to mention something to her about Jack, maybe give her a little talk on the importance of cutting apron strings.

He fulminated in silence as they stepped outside the restaurant, where the swing towards autumn was felt in the chill in the air. Francesca was making conversation, chatting about a television programme she had watched the night before. Normally, he would have teased her by adopting a viewpoint he knew would get under her skin and they would have a heated debate, even if the topic only happened to be something trivial that had taken place in one of those ridiculous reality shows she was addicted to. By the time they finished discussing the subject her cheeks would be flushed and her eyes dancing with pleasure at the sparring.

Not tonight.

He waited until there was a pause in the conversation, then inserted silkily, 'You never told me, how is Jack? Is he between women at the moment? Or is he still dancing around the one with the kid?'

Startled by the abrupt change of conversation and the tone of his voice, Francesca glanced at Angelo's hard profile and felt her stomach flip over. She so much wanted this evening to go well but had to concede that she had ambushed her own good intentions from the start by antagonising him with her foolish speculations about wanting to talk to him, wanting to know whether he would ever see her without sex being the primary objective. She linked her

arm through his and attempted to smooth the situation back
to where she wanted it to be.

'I know you don't approve of Jack's lifestyle, Angelo,
but he's happy and I have to say most of his women do
remain friends with him.'

'That's by the by,' Angelo dismissed. 'Isn't it about time
he grew up and stopped depending on you for advice? If
you want my opinion, the relationship you have with him
is entirely unhealthy. How is he ever going to have the
strength to do anything on his own if he knows that you'll
always be there, picking up the pieces and dusting him
down?' He refrained from voicing his primary concern,
which was that Jack might have far too much influence over
what she thought for her own good.

Francesca was bewildered. 'I'm not always around picking up the pieces,' she refuted hotly. 'Jack confides in me
as a friend—'

'And offers advice to you as a friend as well, I assume?
A little word here, a little insinuation there? Has Jack been
saying anything to you that would make you dissatisfied
with what we have? I can feel your mood, Francesca. Has
he been spinning you tales of what you should expect out
of this? Maybe steering you towards something like commitment? Because, if that's the case, then I can tell you
straight away that it's not going to work. What we have is
sex and there's no point spoiling a perfectly good situation
by entertaining thoughts that it might lead anywhere.'

Francesca was winded by the onslaught and barely had
time to recover before he was continuing, voice hard.
'There's no mileage in thinking that I will end up the fool
that I was three years ago, because I won't.' They had
reached his place and she followed in a daze as he slipped
his hand into his trouser pocket to withdraw his keys so
that he could unlock his front door.

He flicked on the light in the hallway and, without looking at her, strode into the kitchen so that he could pour himself a glass of something stiff and strong.

'Oh, commitment is the furthest thing from my mind.' Francesca couldn't stop a note of bitterness from entering her voice. 'Anyway, Jack would never preach to anyone about commitment. He develops strong allergic reactions just at the sound of the word.'

'So what's bugging you?'

Francesca recognised the disgruntlement in his voice and told herself that she had no one to blame. It was her own damn fault. She had made a conscious and adult decision to take what she could get while she could, knowing full well that it was an ill-conceived decision, but allowing her heart to rule supreme over her head. Every choice had a price and the selfish ones carried the highest stakes. She wouldn't think about that. Not just yet. She went up behind him and slipped her arms around his waist, feeling some of the tension seep out of his body.

'Can't a girl have an off moment?' She rested her head on his shoulder and then stood on tiptoe so that she could kiss the back of his neck.

Angelo laughed and turned around. He pulled her in to him and smiled. 'When she's in my company? How is it possible to have an off moment when in the company of Angelo Falcone?'

And now his tension had completely evaporated, like rain on a hot summer's day. The power of physical contact. At least as far as he was concerned, it made a nonsense of words. He didn't want to hear hesitancy or doubt in her voice. He wanted her to be upbeat, cheerful and in a state of constant excitement. That had been the bargain.

'You're right. It's impossible. After all, isn't Ar

Falcone the most charismatic man in the universe? The most intelligent? The sexiest?'

'A cynic might think that you're being sarcastic but thankfully I'm no cynic. At least, not at the moment.' He kissed her, a light, teasing kiss that evolved into a hungry demand, and felt her body weaken against him.

'Shall we continue this in my bedroom?' he asked softly, breaking off to tuck a few strands of hair behind her ears.

'A bed might be more comfortable than the kitchen floor,' Francesca agreed.

They made it up to the bedroom in double speed. By now she was as familiar with his house as she was with her own, although the familiarity was only skin deep. She knew the format of its layout but since they rarely did anything normal inside it, like flop around with cups of coffee or watch television or even sit in some of the chairs with a good book or a newspaper on a Sunday morning, it still had the feel of a very nice, very comfortable hotel. The most intimate thing she did there, aside from make love, was have a shower.

She had also put candles in his bedroom, ignoring his objections that they were a potential fire hazard. Atmosphere, she had told him. Nothing was as wonderfully atmospheric as candles flickering in the dark. And scented ones were even better. Every so often she replaced them and had been amused when, a couple of weeks back, she had discovered that he had added one or two to the collection.

She got undressed as he carefully lit them one by one and she felt a lump gather in her throat. It seemed strangely romantic in a union that was devoid of all romance.

She was out of her clothing by the time his ritual lighting of the candles was over and Angelo turned and looked at her, marvelling at the lithe, graceful lines of her body. Full breasts, perfectly moulded and topped with large rose-coloured nipples, a stomach that owed nothing to exercise and everything to her gene pool, slender hips and legs that were as supple as a gazelle's. Any wonder she still had such a hold over him? What man in his right mind wouldn't want to make love to a woman as exquisite as that over and over again?

He stood where he was and unbuttoned his shirt. His skin felt hot. He tugged the shirt off and tossed it on the floor, then his trousers and boxers followed suit. He was heavily aroused and it amused him to see the way her eyes drifted to his erect manhood. He could almost hear the little catch in her breath. He took it in one hand and tantalised her by slowly pleasuring himself.

Without saying anything, Francesca moved to the bed and lay down, stretching out provocatively and curling her fingers around the wrought iron railings of the bed head.

Angelo moved towards her, hand still on his stiffened member, until he was standing right over her.

'Oh, the games people play.' He laughed softly, watching as she moved forward so that she could push his hand away and replace it with her mouth. He had never known a woman who was so adept at giving him pleasure, just as she was giving him pleasure now, licking and sucking the massive swell of his erection.

He plunged his fingers into her hair and arched back, knowing that he was only a hair's breadth away from spilling his seed. He had to exercise the utmost control, making sure that his breathing was deep and even. He tugged her gently away when he was actually aching from the need to ejaculate.

'Oh, no, my beautiful little witch.' Their eyes met and tangled in the half light. 'I want to savour every last inch of you before I get there… I want you to hold on to the iron rails and don't let go, whatever I do…'

'Sounds ominous. Should I be scared?'

'Only if you're scared of going to Heaven…'

'That's a big promise.'

'And I'm a man who always keeps his.' He straddled her and she held fast to the rails of the bed head. Her breasts pouted up at him, the rosy nipples swollen and sensitive, but first he kissed her, leaning down and supporting himself on either side of her with his hands. His kiss was hot and urgent and her body arched up until she could feel his member rubbing against her. Lord, but how she wanted him! Her body felt weak and helplessly driven.

She wrapped her arms around him to pull him down and he tutted into her ear.

'No cheating, now.'

'I have to touch you, Angelo!'

'In due course… Now, am I going to have to tie you up? I'm not averse to a little bondage.'

A hot surge of excitement flooded her and she grinned at him, her breathing quick and unsteady.

'Oh, you keep handcuffs on the premises, do you? Very kinky, Mr Falcone. I wonder what your mother would have to say about that!'

'Not handcuffs, my little darling. But I do have a wide assortment of silk ties.' He nibbled her neck while she writhed under him, desperate for him to press himself against her.

'Silk ties sound like fun.' Francesca couldn't believe what she was saying but her trust in him was so utterly complete. Where no other man would ever be permitted to venture, she flung open the door to him. He wrapped silk ties around her wrists, so loosely that she could pull free of them at any time, not that she wanted to.

Then, inch by inch, he explored her body, starting with her shoulders and working his way down to her breasts. He suckled on them, tugging the tips gently with his teeth and drawing moans of pleasure from her. Instead of rushing him to continue, she was constrained by the ties to submit to this leisurely exploration. His tongue trailed along her stomach, circling her belly button as his hands smoothed sensuously along her sides, then up to massage her breasts, to prime them for yet more erotic pleasure. His tongue rasping over her nipples dragged a groan out of her—a husky, animal sound that she couldn't believe she had made.

'This isn't fair!' Francesca panted, and he stopped in the middle of his sensory feasting on her breasts to glance up at her.

'But are you enjoying yourself?'

'You know I am! But I want you!'

'And I want you too,' he confirmed smugly. 'In the meantime, lie back and have fun...' He grinned at her. 'Think of England!'

Francesca thought of anything but England. In fact, she didn't think at all. She just obeyed his command for her to have fun although it bordered on the impossible not to drag herself free of her silken trap when he parted her legs and inserted himself between them so that he could breathe in the sweetness of her femininity. A few flicks of his tongue and she was quivering and moving against his mouth, urging him on with her body.

Angelo cupped her buttocks with his hands and brought her up to meet his questing tongue, which he slid rhythmically over her sensitised bud. He could feel it throbbing. He knew her body as well as he knew his own, knew when the time was right for him to cease pleasuring her in that manner because she needed him to thrust into her or else she would tip over the edge into her own private climax.

Francesca's body welcomed him in, moving in the same rhythm as his as he took her to a shuddering orgasm that left her trembling in its aftermath.

He undid the silk ties and massaged her wrists.

'Look at them, they're ruined,' Francesca said, turning the ties over in her hands.

'Well worth the money I spent on them.' Angelo grinned and felt like a young man who had just ravished the woman of his dreams. He cupped her breast with his hand, a gesture of possession, and Francesca's stomach went into tiny, painful knots. She edged away and lay on her side, primly tugging the quilt up so that it covered her.

'I think I'm going to have a bath now.' It was the last thing she felt like doing when her body was still so pleasantly slumberous and content, but she had to talk to him and talking would be better fully dressed.

Angelo gave a little frown of consternation. 'Why?'

'Because I want to get cleaned up. You know…'

'No, I don't.' He was feeling it again. That little nagging apprehension that had been there at the restaurant. He told himself that he was mistaken, that no woman who had made love as passionately as she just had would ever have anything to say to him that might cause him concern. 'But if you really feel you need to shower, then go ahead. Care for me to come and help you?'

'I think tonight I might manage the exercise on my own.'

When she emerged, she was fully dressed and she saw his eyebrows raise in surprise.

'We need to talk. I know talking isn't part of…this deal we have, but…'

He patted a space on the bed next to him and Francesca remained where she was. 'Why don't you get dressed? I can't talk to you when—when you're naked under the covers.'

Angelo looked at her carefully. He heard the edgy wariness in her voice and he knew what was coming, what this little talk was going to be about.

'Give me five minutes to have a shower. If you like, you can go downstairs and make us both a cup of coffee. I'll take mine black.' He strode past her towards the bathroom and shut the door. He leaned against the door, eyes shut, and contemplated what he was going to do. Sitting back and allowing her to spin him a story about walking away because she had finally decided she wanted more than he could give wasn't an option. That carried the nasty odour of how things had been played out the last time around. Not quite the same but close enough. The walking out bit would certainly be the same.

No, he would take the bull by the horns and dismiss her. It was always going to come to that in the end and if he was taken by surprise it was only because he wasn't quite ready for her to leave his life. He still enjoyed making love to her, but he wasn't going to cling on and try to persuade her to change her mind. In fact, he would rather have walked barefoot on a bed of hot coals than allow his emotions to formulate arguments his head didn't want.

He turned on the shower, making sure that it was as cold as his body could stand, and afterwards stuck on some jeans and a tee shirt. She was no longer in the bedroom. He went downstairs to find that the coffee had been made and she was sipping hers at the kitchen table. Next to her was her bag, a clear indication of the nature of the chat she had in mind.

'I have something to say, Angelo, and it's not going to be easy...'

Angelo didn't say anything. There was a buzzing in his ears and he didn't know whether it was from rage that she intended to pull the same stunt on him again or frustration that he had let himself walk into a situation which had managed to bring him to this impasse. He strolled with his mug in his hand towards the chair facing her and sat down, looping his foot around the other chair so that he could drag it towards him. He was the picture of a man utterly at ease, sprawled on his chair, feet indolently stretched out on the chair he had pulled towards him.

'Then let me help you along, Francesca,' he drawled. 'We had a deal and the deal hasn't changed. The deal is *never* going to change. If you've suddenly decided that you need to tweak the rules, then you're barking up the wrong tree. I want you for one thing and one thing only.' The buzzing in his head was louder but his voice was perfectly calm, cold even.

'Yes, I know that…'

'No,' Angelo cut in coolly, 'I don't think you do. Like every other woman under the sun, you start off with the right intentions but somewhere along the line the rules of the game begin to get a little unpalatable and you decide that it might be a good idea to change them—'

'That's not true! You don't even know what I'm going to say!' And beating about the bush wasn't going to do her any favours but the closer she came to telling him the truth the more she shied away from the hideous complications it would involve.

'I don't have to,' Angelo told her indifferently. He sipped the coffee. He had been in control of their little fling and he intended to be in control of its demise. But there was a leaden feeling inside him that made him feel slightly sick. 'At any rate, it doesn't matter what you have to say. I won't lie, I was enjoying our little romps…' *Romps* seemed a particularly good word, reducing what they had to strictly sex but reducing it in a way that left no room for dignity or glamour. It was a basic, dismissive description and he saw the way she flinched in response. 'But all good things come to an end and I just want to smooth the path for you by telling you that I'm more than happy to part company with you, no hard feelings. There. Have I helped you out at all?'

'It's not as easy as that...'

'Don't make a drama out of nothing, Francesca. It's actually very easy.' He looked at her impassively, noted the tremulous quivering of her mouth and steeled himself against the temptation to ask her questions, in fact to show any interest at all.

Was that what she was doing? Making a drama out of nothing? If only he knew! If only he knew that the low dosage contraceptive pill she had been assiduously taking had been too late to prevent the baby growing inside her, the product of that very first time they had made love spontaneously and unprotected, weeks and weeks ago. It was only today, when she'd realised that her breasts were feeling heavier than usual and more sensitive than they normally did, that the period she should have had during the gap in the little white tablets had been noticeable only by its non-appearance, that she had been feeling queasy at the sight of coffee and the smell of fried foods—disastrous for a chef and something she had ignored to start with—only now had she turned cold at the possible nightmare situation she might be facing.

She knew that she should have called him as soon as she'd discovered the awful truth. At least then he would have had time to prepare himself for when they met. Instead, she had decided to put off the dreaded confrontation. She would have her last memory of him, something to treasure for the rest of her life, and then she would tell him. Now, here she was and she still hadn't told him. She felt like someone staring up the face of Mount Everest and trying to work out how best to reach the summit without dying in the process.

'You don't understand. If you'd just let me explain...' She wondered, sickly, what format these explanations would take. Perhaps, *You're going to be a daddy soon,* or maybe just a blunt, *Life as you know it is about to go into free fall.*

'There's nothing to explain,' Angelo interrupted. 'And I'm not interested in explanations.' He stood up and politely waited for her to do the same.

Francesca stood too and stared at him across the width of the table. She would tell him about the pregnancy, but maybe not just yet, because what good would telling him do? She was still in the position she had been in three years ago. Telling him would present him with an insoluble problem. She felt sick with the worry of it all. In this day and age insoluble problems such as the one she was dealing with had an obvious solution that came under the heading of abortion, but Francesca would not even contemplate going down that road. Whatever wrong turns she had taken in her life had been of her own choosing or at least her own foolishness, and she had always taken responsibility for the consequences. That wasn't going to change now. And besides...she loved him. True love was unselfish, she told herself, as she blindly gathered up her handbag. The unselfish thing to do would be to spare him the knowledge of the time bomb waiting to destroy his life and his career.

'If it's all right, I'll just call a taxi,' she whispered, fishing in the bag for her mobile phone.

'No need for that. I'll give you a lift back. Like I said, no hard feelings.' He even managed a smile and for Francesca that was worse because it was so very impersonal.

He drove her back to her house in unbroken silence. The

temptation to tell him what was going on was overpowering, but hard on the heels of temptation came the icy blast of reality—the position she would be putting him in, the consequences he would be forced to deal with.

The silent drive finally came to an end and he turned to her. 'Good luck with your catering business, Francesca. I'll make sure to put in a good word for you.'

'There's no need…'

'Call it for services rendered.' It was a cheap shot but the tip of the iceberg when it came to what he was feeling. Yes, he had been the one to do the discarding and, no, it felt no better now than it had three years ago when the shoe had been on the other foot. He could see from her face that the dart had hit bull's-eye and loathed himself for delivering it. Too late now, and he wasn't going to apologise anyway.

'That's…below the belt.'

'It's the unvarnished truth.' He shrugged.

'I'm sorry.' She took a deep breath and weathered the shuttered, dark face impassively staring back at her. 'I didn't think that it would end this way.'

'Apologies accepted, although we both enjoyed the ride so none are due.'

'I don't think I'll be staying on in London.' She gave a high, brittle laugh.

'No?' He sounded mildly, but only mildly, interested. 'Don't feel obliged to leave on account of me.'

Francesca nodded. Conversation had dried up. Angelo was making no attempt to extend himself beyond the formalities of answering her questions. There was the faintest semblance of boredom on his beautiful face.

Her notions about passion fizzling out conveniently, leaving her cleansed and free to move on with her life, had been a terrible illusion, and her selfishness in agreeing to sleep with him for the gratification it gave her now seemed a terminally grave misjudgement.

Angelo watched as she walked up towards her front door. He didn't wait to see her go in. By the time Francesca had reached her sitting room and collapsed into one of the sofas, he was already three blocks away from her house and heading out of London. At this time of night the roads were empty. Once on the motorway, he revved the powerful car and ate up the miles to nowhere.

Not that the purposeless three-hour drive managed to do much for his state of mind.

Nor, for that matter, did the ensuing two weeks of working like a beast. He buried himself in work, pushing himself to the limits, knowing that people were looking at him oddly and wondering what the hell was going on. He had no desire to fill any of them in. In fact, there was a certain amount of perverse satisfaction to be had from noting the way his staff scurried out of his way when they saw him coming. They sensed his black mood and made sure to avoid it whenever they could. Just as well. It was as he was preparing to leave on the Friday that his mobile rang. Without any identifying name popping up for him to ascertain who the caller was, he very nearly let it ring. He had plans for the evening which included too much whisky for his own good, but in the end curiosity got the better of him.

He recognised the voice before the caller identified himself and he felt every nerve in his body tense.

'What do you want?' He steamrollered his way through the opening apologetic platitudes, getting straight to the point. He flicked back his wrist and wondered what Jack was doing calling him after ten on a Friday. If the man thought that he could scramble a few favours from him on the back of Francesca's affair then he could think again.

'I know you're a very busy man, Mr Falcone…'

'Yes. I am. So you'll excuse me when I tell you to get to the point.'

'Could we meet, mate?'

'What for?' Silence greeted his direct question. 'Has Francesca put you up to this? Because if she thinks that I'm going to be a soft touch for money because we happened to sleep together, then you can run along and tell her from me that she's barking up the wrong tree.'

'Els doesn't know that I'm calling you. In fact, I think there's a good chance she'd kill me if she did.'

Against his will, Angelo was intrigued. It was weak but what harm was there in meeting the man? If money was the root of the phone call, whatever the packaging, then wasn't it best to make it perfectly clear from the word go that none would be forthcoming?

'I can see you tonight. Take it or leave it.' Intrigued but not so intrigued that he was going to make any spaces in his diary. He named a bar in Kensington. 'I'll be there in half an hour. I intend to stay for one drink and I won't wait.'

He pressed the end button on his phone, cutting off any attempt at negotiation.

He'd spent the past two weeks itching for a fight, he thought grimly. Maybe now he was about to get one.

CHAPTER NINE

'You did *what*?' Francesca's eyes widened in horror. To be greeted at eight in the morning with a bombshell was like strolling along an open field only to find that you'd stepped off the edge of a cliff. No, been *pushed off* the edge of a cliff. And the perpetrator of the crime was standing in her hall, looking for all the world as though his casual announcement was on the same level as imparting some trivial bit of information about the price of shellfish.

Jack braced himself to weather the storm.

'Told him about the pregnancy.'

'How *could* you, Jack? How could you go and betray me like that?' She spun around and went into the sitting room where she could collapse into one of the chairs and bury her head in her arms. She was aware that he had followed her in but she just wished he would go. Her heart was pounding as she tried to grapple with the fallout from this revelation. What would Angelo do? He would be furious. No, furious wouldn't even begin to describe how he would feel. She groaned.

'I never betrayed you.'

'No?' Francesca looked at him. 'And what would you call sneaking around behind my back and spilling the beans to Angelo? When you *knew* that I'd decided not to say anything. Not yet, anyway. Would you call it an act of love?'

'I'd call it looking out for you, actually.'

'And your notion of looking out for me means that I'm going to have to leave—'

'You mean run away?' Jack sat on one of the chairs, hunkered over. 'Tried that one already, haven't you?'

Francesca shot him a baleful look. 'What else did you tell him?'

'Nothing. Just that you were pregnant. He needs to know.'

'He needs to know just like he needs a hole in the head.'

Jack ignored the outburst. 'You were going to tell him, Els. You know you were.'

'And he made it clear that he didn't want me to tell him anything! He wanted me to walk away, so I did!'

'But it wasn't what you intended,' he persisted in the face of her glowering self-justification. 'It's wrong and you know it. You can't keep him in the dark about something as important as that.'

'I wouldn't be the first to keep a man in the dark when the situation is hopeless.'

'Which doesn't make it right. Okay, maybe if…if you feared for your safety, then fair enough, but it's not like that.'

'How do you know what it's like, Jack? If you think there's anything sentimental between us then you're living in cloud cuckoo land. Angelo offered me a proposition. Sleep with him or else walk away.'

'I know. And you chose to have a relationship…'

'I *chose* to have sex with him,' Francesca said tightly, reducing it to the most basic terms possible. She had to keep thinking straight. It was the only way to extricate herself from the mess. She didn't want Jack to start harping on about her feelings for Angelo. For someone who had structured his life around non-involvement, he had a very healthy set of romantic notions, and one of them was that because she loved Angelo then everything would surely be all right. In her more generous moments she had found this trait endearing. Now she just found it insufferable and a breach of her privacy.

'And now that this has happened, well, it's my problem and I'm going to deal with it and if that means *running away* then, yes, I'm going to run away, and if I can't trust you not to betray me *again*, then I'm going to have to leave without a forwarding address.'

'Don't be daft. How are you going to do that? You own a house, you own a catering business...'

Francesca's mind feverishly took off down the road of practicalities. Where exactly would she go? And if Angelo wanted to find her, then he would. It would be easy. She would have to sell the house, sell off all the kitchen equipment and, even if she handed it over to a lawyer to do, he would still be able to trace her through that route. She couldn't bear to look at Jack. It was the first time since they had been kids that any major disagreement had arisen between them.

While she was still grappling with the enormity of what lay ahead, Jack was again speaking, his voice oddly firm and controlled.

'You can't run away. You've run away too many times and now you've got to stop. I wouldn't have gone to see him if I thought that you were happy with your decision...'

'I have been very happy with my decision!' Francesca said hotly.

Jack's voice was as calm as hers had been vehement. 'No, you haven't. You've been miserable and now it's affecting the pregnancy. You know what the doctor said. Much more stress and you run the risk of miscarrying. Is that what you want?'

No, it wasn't. She might not have expected or wanted to be pregnant with Angelo's child but, now that she was, she felt intensely happy about it. It was about the only thing she *did* feel happy about. It was selfish, but there was a strong sense of wanting this bit of him for ever.

'Well, thank you very much for introducing yet more stress for me to cope with.'

'You need to start being honest.' He stood up and brushed himself down. It had been a late night. When he thought back to Angelo's reaction to what he had said—the disbelief followed swiftly by cold, angry shut-down—he could understand why she now felt inclined to take off. The man was, frankly, intimidating, but taking off was not the answer and he was convinced that the guilt she blithely dismissed would eat away at her until she ended up in hospital. If she had never intended to fill him in then he might have remained silent but she had meant to and had chickened out at the last moment, and had then wrapped up her cowardice in lots of flowery packaging of *being mature* and *thinking of the impact it would have on his life* and *wanting to spare him the unfair anguish of having to deal with a mistake she had made,* as though she had been solely responsible for the situation.

After he had met Angelo he had headed back to his local pub and drowned any niggling doubts he had had in a few pints of lager. Lord only knew how the pair of them were going to get it together to do justice to the job they had for later that evening. Give it another week and the kids they used would be rising up in arms and staging a mutiny.

'Where are you going?' Francesca demanded, standing up and then sitting back down when she was overcome by a wave of nausea and dizziness.

At once Jack was by her side. 'I'll stay if you want, Els.'

'Was he very angry?' she asked in a small voice and the slight hesitation provided her with an answer. 'God,' she moaned, curling into him, forgetting the fact that he had become the bad guy.

'Talk it over with him. He was pretty angry, yes, but I did tell him that you had wanted to say something. You can sort something out...at least then your conscience will be clear...' Philosophical pearls of wisdom had never been his forte and he lapsed into silence, stroking her back until he felt she was calm enough for him to pull back.

'I suppose you thought you were doing the right thing,' Francesca said grudgingly and Jack breathed a sigh of relief at this little crumb of conciliation. Before she had any opportunity to resume her attack, he decided to take advantage of the temporary laying down of arms.

'Let me get you something to eat before I go,' he suggested. 'I could whip something up. Some good old-fashioned eggy bread, maybe?'

Francesca made a face. 'I can't stomach the thought of fried food. I'll grab myself a few crackers when you've gone.'

'What about this job tonight?'

'I went shopping yesterday and everything's in the fridges.' She looked at him despairingly and he nodded.

'Okay. But no running away when my back's turned. Fair enough if he doesn't get in touch...'

Shying away from the thought of a vengeful Angelo, Francesca clung to this nonsense possibility like a man clinging on to a lifebelt in high seas. The thought that Angelo might decide to walk away from the horrendous situation confronting him was very appealing.

And if he did contact her...

She would deal with it. She could spend the rest of her life running but in the end she wouldn't be able to hide and, even if she did succeed in disappearing, what good would it do in the long term? Sooner or later the baby would grow into a child and the child would grow into an adult who wanted answers to questions.

It was almost a sense of relief to know that the decision had pretty much been taken out of her hands. All she had to do now was wait.

Not long, if Angelo had his way, but he knew that he had to curb the urge to drive over to her house immediately and lay into her.

His phone rang for the third time that morning, even though it had only just gone nine and, knowing who it was, he snatched it up and said, without bothering with formalities, 'What do you want?'

There had been five messages on his answering machine when he had returned the night before. All from Georgina. Then three calls this morning, all of which he let the answering machine get. He certainly didn't feel inclined to be civil to anyone, least of all his ex-girlfriend, who had disappeared only to resurface just when he needed no distractions.

Pregnant.

Angelo had barely been able to take it in when Jack had launched his bombshell. In fact, it had initially crossed his mind that it might have been some kind of ruse to extract money from him, even though he knew her well enough to know that that would not be her style. The self-delusion hadn't lasted long. The man had been utterly serious. There had been no mistaking his body language and there had been no mistaking the simple truth, which was that he had not come to see him with Francesca's permission.

Which meant that she had had no intention of telling him about the pregnancy. The treachery involved in her silence had rendered him speechless. He had listened to Jack stutter out one or two excuses on her behalf but he had barely heard them. He had left rather than be fed with further rubbish along those lines. Had returned home to find his answering machine blinking at him.

'I wondered whether we could meet, Angelo. There's something I have to talk to you about.'

Meeting Georgina was the last thing he wanted to do. Nor did he care for the barely hidden smugness in her voice. Had she found out about his affair with Francesca? More than likely. London was a big place but not so big in certain circles that word might not have got round. They could have been spotted at any time and the grapevine in the city was as lush and vibrant as any grapevine anywhere else.

And if she had known about the relationship, then it was also possible that she knew of its demise. Was she planning a comeback? Angelo's mouth curved into a grim smile of contempt. He could barely remember that faraway time when he had been contemplating marriage to her, content to let common sense dictate his judgements. In fact, he could barely remember a time before Francesca had exploded once again into his life, bringing back all the confusion he had thought well left behind.

'I have nothing to say to you, Georgina.'

'Oh, but I have something to say to *you*.' The smugness was right out in the open now and Angelo allowed his feelings to get the better of him. Damned if he was going to let her have free rein to gloat over things that were none of her business.

'Do you now?' he enquired coldly. 'Well, I'm not interested and, in fact, I'm on my way out to see Francesca. So if you'll excuse me...' He hung up, almost expecting to hear the insistent ringing of the phone as she tried to reconnect, but the house was silent.

He left before the silence could be broken and forced himself not to drive like a madman over to her house. The situation felt almost dreamlike, surreal. With the ease of habit, he began thinking about the consequences of the situation. She would have kept this baby to herself because, at the end of the day, whatever good sex they had shared, it wasn't enough. It hadn't been enough three years ago and it wasn't enough now. But she was having his baby and her feelings would have to be secondary, whether she liked it or not.

His jaw clenched in anger and he breathed in slowly and deeply, taking his time in the Saturday morning traffic.

It was mid-morning by the time he reached her place and he almost expected to find that she had gone out, but no. He rang the doorbell and heard the sound of footsteps behind the closed door.

Francesca took a deep breath, hand on the door knob. She had been dreading this moment, knowing it would come, and knowing, as well, that he wouldn't give her any advance warning. No time for her to prepare herself. It wouldn't have mattered at any rate. She was as prepared now as she would ever be.

She opened the door and her courage failed her at the sight of his grim, implacable face.

'Come in.' She turned around and began walking towards the sitting room. She only faced him when they were both in the room, at which point she had no choice, but that didn't mean that she was any less afraid. Her heart was thumping inside her and she felt sweaty.

'Would you like something to drink?' she asked, clasping her hands together on her lap and leaning forward.

Angelo's mouth twisted. 'Bit late in the day for polite exchanges, don't you think? Bearing in mind that you were going to disappear off the face of the earth with my baby?'

Francesca blanched. 'I...I...wasn't going to disappear off the face of the earth...'

'No? Just duck out of sight? Call it whatever you want to call it, Francesca, but you had no intention of telling me, did you?' He clenched his fists to stop himself from hitting something. 'How dare you,' he said coldly, 'think that you could keep my child away from me?'

'I *did* intend to tell you, Angelo, but, if you recall, you weren't exactly receptive when we last met!'

'And you didn't think that the information was important enough to make a stand!'

'I didn't think that it would do any good telling you!'

Angelo stared at her as though she had taken leave of her senses, stared at her until a soft pink glow invaded her cheeks. 'Run that by me again,' he said with silky threat. 'I'm struggling to understand how having my child and keeping it a secret would benefit me.'

'Look at your life, Angelo! You know where you're going. You like to be in control. What happened was my fault. I got swept away that first time we... Well, anyway, I wasn't using any protection on that one occasion, I lied to you when I said I was, and now I'm pregnant. I didn't think it was right for you to spend the rest of your life paying for the mistake.'

'And it didn't occur to you that I should have been given the choice?'

'Yes, of course it did! Which is why I went to see you, to tell you, but you wanted me out and I realised that leaving was probably the best way.'

'Handy conclusion, wasn't it? Any time you had a struggle with your conscience you could always remind yourself that you had tried, after all, given it your best shot.' He moved to stand in front of her, his towering anger sheathing his body like a steel glove.

But fighting the anger. She could tell from the way his jaw clenched. He was forcibly biting back what he wanted to say. Her mind played with the pleasing fantasy of how peaceful life would have been if she had really just run away. At least for a few years. Then she remembered the stress that had been eating away at her.

'There's no point laying into me, Angelo,' she said quietly. 'Now that you know, I shall try and include you in our child's life. I understand that you might want to help support him, or her, financially, but I just want you to know upfront that I won't accept any money from you for myself.'

Angelo gave an incredulous laugh and moved to one of the chairs, where he promptly sat down, crossing his long legs. 'That's very generous of you, Francesca. Sadly, it falls somewhat short of what I had in mind.'

'What did you have in mind?' Francesca asked faintly. She unconsciously placed one hand protectively on her stomach.

'Something a little more…shall we say, involved?'

'What do you mean by that?' Visions of him showing up every afternoon on her doorstep flooded her mind. In the space of a few seconds she had a blinding vision of him always being around, a stranger with whom she had once shared a fleeting past, a stranger she would continually struggle to fall out of love with. It would never work.

'I mean,' Angelo explained patiently but ruthlessly, 'I don't intend to be sidelined into visitor mode. I didn't ask to be catapulted into fatherhood but, now that that's the reality, I intend to deal with it.'

'Deal with it?' Francesca didn't like the sound of that. 'It's not a knotty work problem, Angelo!'

'No,' he agreed smoothly. 'But, like every other situation in life, there is a solution and the solution I have in mind will be a permanent one.'

'I won't let you take this baby away from me!' She stood up, trembling with a mixture of apprehension and anger and immediately sat back down. 'You may have a lot of money but there's no court in this land that would tear a mother apart from her child because of that!'

'Nor should there be. Do you really think that I would be monstrous enough to suggest such a thing? I was raised in a very secure family environment, both parents very active on the upbringing front. I would never contemplate splitting a mother from her child to pursue fatherhood on my own.'

'What then?'

'We will be married.'

Four words dropped into the silence like time bombs. Time, for a few seconds, seemed to stand completely still and the colour drained from her face. She shook her head slowly, in a daze.

This time, Angelo thought, sensing the sour whiff of refusal, there would be no running out on him. He would marry her for the sake of his child if he had to haul her up the aisle kicking and screaming. It should have made him feel enraged and impotent at the situation thrust upon him, but he found himself contentedly watching her squirm. Why was that? He skirted over the business of trying to work that one out and maintained his silence.

'That's a crazy suggestion.' Francesca tried a laugh which stalled in her throat. 'People don't just get married because of a pregnancy. Not in this day and age.'

'Maybe that's what's wrong with the world.' Angelo shrugged. 'However, I'm not one of those people. I don't walk away from my responsibilities in the hope that someone else will come along and pick up the pieces.'

'I wasn't asking you to run away from your responsibilities!' Francesca cried. 'I already told you that you can have as much input as you like into what goes on!' Already she could see the huge complications that would arise from that, but none of those complications would rival the ones raised by her marrying him.

'Not good enough,' Angelo pointed out patiently. 'What happens when you find another man? Do I resign myself to sitting back in the shadows while my child calls another man *Daddy*?'

'This is ludicrous! I haven't even had the baby yet and you're talking about what might or might not happen in the years to come!'

'I find that predicting potential problems is the safest way to circumnavigate them.'

Francesca tried to feel angry but this philosophy was so typical of him that she was almost tempted to smile. What some would describe as controlling, Angelo would always describe as practical. Right now, he was behaving in the most practical way he could imagine, because in his head he was already predicting the possible consequences of acting in any other manner. And, like it or not, he was part Italian. The thought of his child being raised without his name would cause him severe problems. Francesca wondered why she hadn't foreseen this dilemma but she had been so wrapped up in the enormity of trying to work out the suddenly altered logistics of her own life that she simply hadn't paused to think ahead.

'You don't understand, Angelo. I can't do the wife thing with you.'

'I don't believe I heard myself giving you a choice.'

'Which doesn't mean that you're going to get your own way. I just…I just can't marry you…whatever the situation. I'm sorry…'

'What a noble little thing you are!'

Angelo and Francesca both looked around at precisely the same time and there she was, standing framed in the doorway, perky in a small, dove-grey suit with the requisite string of pearls and ivory clutch bag. Georgina was going for the cool, sophisticated look. Not a strand of hair was out of place.

'Sorry to intrude, but the front door was open. I did knock…' she strolled elegantly into the sitting room and then found a spot by the bay window, against which she proceeded to perch '…but no one heard. Obviously too absorbed…chatting.'

Angelo was the first to speak. 'What the hell are you doing here, Georgina?' His voice was perfectly modulated, politely interested even, but there was a thread of steel underlying it that sent a chill racing down Francesca's spine. Georgina, who was casually glancing around the room, seemed oblivious to any threat. In fact, Francesca thought, she appeared utterly at ease and quite pleased with herself.

'I did try calling you, Angelo—' she looked at him sorrowfully '—but you didn't see fit to return any of my calls, even though I *did* try to make it clear that I had something of importance to tell you.'

'And, as I made perfectly clear to you when you did get through to me, I wasn't interested in whatever you had to say.'

Georgina treated this with a tight, vindictive little smile. Neither of them had heard the front door opening and Francesca wondered how long the other woman had been in the house. Had she been standing by the sitting room door, listening to every word of the conversation?

'Well, you should be because I can tell you why your little slapper can't get too involved with you, whatever the situation.' For the first time she directed her glance to Francesca, who was watching her warily. 'Oh, dear. Pregnant.' She shook her head ruefully. 'Bit of a slip-up, Ellie. Or should I say, Francesca?'

'How *dare* you come into my house and insult me?' She

half rose but Angelo was there before her, his face black as thunder. The feeling of events rushing upon him like a steamroller had intensified, but there was one event he intended to do something about.

'Leave. Now.'

'Or else?' Georgina arched her eyebrows. 'What will you do, break off our engagement? I believe you've already done that, Angelo.'

'Oh, but there's so much more that I could do, Georgina,' he said conversationally. He strolled away from her, moving towards the back of Francesca's chair and leaning forward on it, a gesture of intense protectiveness which Georgina didn't fail to notice. Her mouth thinned into a hard, unattractive line but she was still looking at him as though his threats were empty. Francesca could have warned her that if she had any sense at all she would take him seriously. Against her will, she found herself liking the way he was protecting her, making sure that she wasn't tossed to the wolf. It wouldn't change anything but…it felt good.

'Really, Angelo? Like what?'

'Oh, friendships can be such fiendishly fickle things, especially among the rich and beautiful in London. And how demeaning for you were word to get around that you were finding it hard to cope with the misery of rejection, that you were willing to creep around trying to make trouble for me long after the event. You might even find yourself being portrayed as somewhat unbalanced, and the whiff of emotional instability is a major turn-off when it comes to friends, I would have said. No one likes a stalker. '

Some of the confidence was draining away but Georgina still managed to maintain eye contact with him, while Francesca watched in fascinated silence.

'Stalker?' She dropped her eyes and when she next

looked at Angelo it was with contrition. Francesca had never seen such a rapid transformation of facial expression. The woman could have been nominated for an Oscar. 'How could you accuse me of that? Don't you know that I'm only here because I really care about you? And don't want you to be seen as a laughing stock?'

'I have no idea what you're talking about, Georgina, and I don't intend to waste any more time listening to the rantings of a jealous woman.'

'I'm not ranting. Ask your girlfriend about Birmingham and that unfortunate brush with trouble she had. I'm sure she'll only be too happy to tell you what I'm talking about—to fill you in on why exactly she won't be marrying you. Ditched for the second time, Angelo…how degrading for you.' She pushed herself away from the window ledge and slanted a malicious smile at Francesca. 'Well, I'll be off now. Hope you haven't *too* many pieces to pick up, Angelo.' She left as she had entered, in a swirl of elegant complacency.

'Care to tell me what that was all about?' Angelo swung round so that he was facing Francesca.

The house of cards had finally come crashing down. She took a deep breath and met his cool, curious gaze steadily.

'It's something I should have told you a long time ago. When we first met, in fact.'

'Which is?'

'When we met, Angelo, I was a model, working in Europe, a glamorous person without any roots anywhere and no past. Or rather, no past that I felt I could let on to you.' *And the bits that I did fill you in on were creations, little figments I never thought would come back to haunt me…*

'And why would that be?' Angelo had gone very still

but that was only for a moment. Then he walked across to the sofa and sat down.

'That would be because…because of who you are, someone huge and important, moving in all the right circles, mixing with all the right people.' Francesca looked down and was surprised to see that her hands were fluttering nervously on her lap. She didn't *feel* nervous. Just numb. 'The truth is that you never really knew me at all, not the real me.'

'The real you being…?'

'The real me being someone who grew up on one of the roughest council estates in Birmingham, ran with all the wrong people. My mother died from a drugs overdose when I was eight and at sixteen I left school altogether to take care of my father. He was an alcoholic, you see, and—well, somebody had to take care of him so that's what I did. I didn't mind. I was fed up at school anyway. They tried to get me back but I wasn't having any of it. Dad was on benefits and we had enough to just about struggle through.'

Angelo, sitting in complete silence, was trying hard to equate the glamorous model he had met, dated and loved with the person she was now describing. She had always avoided questions about her past but the impression she had left him with was of someone who had lived a fairly ordinary middle-class life. Her revelations now were peeling off the layers of what he thought he knew and exposing the face of someone who was a complete stranger to him and always had been. It left a harshly sour taste in his throat, the sour taste of deception.

'Then Dad died, quite suddenly, and I was left with nothing. I had no education to speak of and, anyway, it was too late for me to think of going back to school. Where I grew up, people didn't think about *going to school*, they thought of ways to get out of it. Even if I had wanted to, I would never have been able to, the peer pressure would have been too much.' Francesca watched Angelo's expressionless face with a sinking heart. Maybe if she had given him some indication in the past that her life had been troubled, then he wouldn't now be sitting there, looking at her as though he was seeing her for the first time.

She took a deep breath and ploughed on. 'Jack was one of the lads in our group and my best friend. I didn't have many girlfriends. They didn't like the way I looked, but Jack and I were mates. It was his suggestion that we just clear off, head for London. It seemed a good idea at the time. I was seventeen by then but I knew that with Dad no longer around, the Social Services might be inclined to get involved and I didn't want to go down that road. The minute Social Services get involved there's a good chance that you'll end up worse off than you were to start with.'

'So you just…took off…'

'We stole a car, something else that seemed a good idea at the time. I didn't think about whether it was right or wrong, it was all just a means to an end. Jack drove.' In retrospect, she could see the craziness of it all but she could remember how she had felt at the time. An orphan, missing her drunken but humorous father, just trying to escape the trap she had seen other girls fall into. The baby at seventeen, then another two years later, the pathetic desperation of endless relationships with abusive boyfriends who disappeared after a few months or a few weeks. The hopelessness.

She just wished that he would say something, even if it was to condemn her, but his silence was complete and, really, wasn't his complete silence damning in itself?

'Of course, we were caught. We hadn't even made it halfway down to London when Jack was picked up for speeding. It didn't take long before we were hauled into a police station and, because there had been a lot in the press about joyriders, we were dealt with pretty harshly. Fingerprints, the lot. I got off because I was just a passenger, but Jack went to prison for six months.'

'And where were you at the time?'

'Back in Birmingham, sleeping rough. I managed to get some casual work at one of the department stores, which was good. When Jack got out, he had changed. He was into drugs.'

Looks or no looks, if Angelo Falcone had met her then, he would have crossed to the other side of the road to avoid her.

'He bummed around for a few months, getting worse and worse…'

'And yet you stuck by him.'

'Because that's what friendship is all about. It was while I was working in that store that I was spotted. It was all a matter of chance. The *Clothes Show* was on and there must have been scouts around. A month later and chances are that I would have ended up in the same place as lots of other girls I knew, pushing a pram at eighteen and dreaming of better things.'

'But you ended up on the other side of the Atlantic, wearing designer clothes…'

And meeting you. 'As soon as I had accumulated some money, I arranged for Jack to be privately treated at a rehab centre. The top one in the country. It's where a lot of my money went.'

Secrecy and lies, Angelo thought.

'He was there for quite a while…and then the balance is, well…'

'History? You paid for him to go on a caterer's course and it turned out to be your refuge as well when you returned to England.'

Francesca nodded and stood up. 'I have a murky past, Angelo, and that might not matter to a lot of people but it would matter to you. The paparazzi would have a field day if they ever found out. Georgina obviously has, but I don't suppose she'll say anything, not after you've issued your warnings…' She couldn't meet his eyes. It was one thing to know the scales had dropped but another thing to actually see it for herself. 'I couldn't get involved with you then and I can't get involved with you now. I certainly can't marry you. I won't be responsible for ruining your reputation.' And his reputation would be ruined. It was all true what he had said about the small but powerful circle of movers and shakers in London. Gossip could spread like wildfire and not only would he personally be tarnished by his contact with her, but he might very well be professionally tarnished as well.

'So all we have to decide is how we deal with this… situation…' No longer travelling down memory lane. She was crisp and businesslike now, not giving him any opportunity for those eyes to express what he thought of her. 'I intend to move away from London, but not too far, perhaps towards Warwick. I know that part of the world and it's a good place to raise a child.' For the first time she looked at him. 'Nothing you can say or do will stop me.'

CHAPTER TEN

FOR the past week Francesca had been on bedrest. She had been feeling sick and light-headed. She couldn't eat. The sight of food, any food, just made her feel sicker. The doctor who had initially warned her that she needed to get her energy levels up had given her a stern warning about the effects of stress on her unborn baby and added some extra spice to his lecture by referring to the vulnerability of women during the first three months of their pregnancy. He had thrown her some scary statistics but by that point Francesca had been too busy thinking about the possibility of losing her baby to pay him much attention.

Bedrest. Dr White had been kind but firm, cutting through her protests about having to work with one raised hand that had stopped her in mid-flow. Bedrest or risk losing the baby—it was as simple as that. And she needed to start eating properly, not just a handful of crackers on the go to stave off nausea.

He had tried to encourage her into chatting about whatever was on her mind but Francesca had just smiled politely at his kindly, encouraging face and assured him that she would take his advice, put her feet up and do something about regulating her diet.

Dr White presented a very sympathetic father figure but Francesca had no desire to spill her feelings out to him or to anyone else. Angelo had walked out of her house, apparently taking her at her word, which was good, and she had not heard a word from him since. Maybe he had gone away, had thought about the ramifications of what she had told him and decided to take the most logical path to dealing with the situation. He was, after all, a highly logical man. He would be in touch, she assumed, in due course, when the need to discuss financial arrangements for the baby became necessary. That wouldn't be for months yet, by which time she intended to be out of London for good, which would be all to his advantage. A child living an hour and a half out of the city was a child he could visit maybe once or twice a month, just enough to salve his conscience and certainly not enough to arouse any suspicions amongst his friends and colleagues. So much for all that talk about wanting to be involved in every aspect of his baby's life. So much for marriage.

Well, could she blame him? He had reacted exactly as she had predicted. Her past had brought the shutters crashing down because, at the end of the day, he just couldn't afford to go out with someone whose credentials were not just average but downright insalubrious.

Francesca, lying flat on her bed, stared up at the ceiling. Next to her was a tray with the remnants of breakfast, brought in by Jack, who had taken to checking up on her three or four times a day and insisting that she eat, like a tyrannical mother hen chivvying a poorly chick into obedience. She half expected that guilt had something to do with that. She hadn't delved into the details of Angelo's reaction to what she had told him, but she had disclosed enough for Jack to realise that there had been no cheerful brushing aside of the past. So now he had taken to fussing around her, even though, with her out of action, he was handling the catering business pretty much on his own, only allowing her to do the books and whatever else she could accomplish from the end of a telephone.

In a couple of hours' time the breakfast tray would be replaced by a lunch tray, complete with a flower in a vase, and some bracing chat about lots of positive things that she should be looking forward to.

Francesca was learning fast how to avoid the concern in his eyes by a barrage of light-hearted patter, just the sort to put his mind at rest, while her own mind relentlessly continued to gnaw over her memories of Angelo. Several times she found herself poised to dial his number. She could always use the excuse of needing to sort things out, but the thought of hearing from his own lips that he wanted nothing further to do with her, that she should cease calling him, that he would do what was necessary but no more, terrified her. In his eyes, she would have been tarnished by her past and she knew that he would not want her to infect his own golden future.

She could feel herself being sucked down the familiar grim path when she became aware of the door downstairs being unlocked and Jack's footsteps coming up the stairs. Earlier than usual.

Francesca wearily plastered a welcoming smile on her face. She made herself go to the chair by her window, which she knew would make him happy because it would show that she was doing a little bit more than just lying down in bed in a maudlin, defeated manner, and was smiling when he strode into the bedroom.

'You're a bit early for lunch, Jack,' she greeted him cheerfully. 'I know you want to feed me up, but a hot meal at ten forty-five in the morning is a bit much!' The smile made her jaws ache. 'Tell me how that job went last night. Did you have to provide waiter service in the end? I've called up the Hamiltons and confirmed that we'll cater for them on the twenty-third and they're going to let us do our own thing with the food, thank Heavens.'

Jack tossed a newspaper on her lap and then stood back

with his arms folded. 'Something in there you need to read.'

Glancing at the headlines, Francesca wondered what the urgency was to read a report on pre-election opinion polls.

'Centre spread,' Jack elaborated. 'And, while you're reading that, there's someone downstairs who wants to see you.'

'Who?' Francesca asked suspiciously.

'The same person who brought me the newspaper. I think your ex might have guessed that in the normal run of things I wouldn't go near a broadsheet. You know I always try to steer clear of any newspaper that has enough pages to wall-paper my lounge.'

'You mean Angelo, don't you?' she asked in rising panic but Jack was already backing out of the door, leaving her at the mercy of a visitor she didn't want to see. Not now. Not yet. Not when she felt sure she was finally getting to grips with everything. Hadn't she made an effort with some make up just this morning? Wasn't that a clear sign that she was turning a corner?

She waited with pounding heart and when Angelo was finally standing in the doorway she found that her voice had seized up. He looked haggard. The smart suit which he should have been wearing mid-morning on a weekday was noticeably absent. In its place was a pair of cords and a faded rugby sweater.

He ran his fingers through his hair and entered the room tentatively.

'How are you?'

'Fine.' Francesca smiled brightly, one of those high watt-age smiles she had mastered to put Jack at ease.

'Jack told me that you've been confined to bedrest by the doctor.'

'It's nothing. Just a bit of raised blood pressure. What are you doing here?'

'We have to talk. Have you read the article?'

'No. What's it about?' Her mind was slowly cranking into gear. A centre spread in a serious newspaper pointed to a declaration of some sort. It wouldn't be simply some business coverage. He wouldn't be looking at her like that, his eyes burning into her, if he wanted her to read something about the latest deal he had done. Her hands were trembling as she turned the pages, finally finding the middle of the newspaper.

Her eyes skimmed over the words on the page, the glaringly big caption at the top, the picture of Angelo taken at some important function and reproduced to show the man in all his eligibility. She felt bright patches of colour flood into her face and, when she finally raised her eyes to meet his, she barely knew what to think. The article was all about her, the significant woman in his life, and nothing had been spared. From the miserable circumstances of her childhood to her rise as a model, it was charted with scrupulous honesty to detail. His intentions were entirely honourable, the spread ran; the man presumed to be one of the country's most eligible bachelors was going to hitch his wagon to a woman who came from the wrong side of the tracks.

'I don't understand…'

'What's there not to understand?' Angelo said thickly. 'You look thin. Is that normal? Shouldn't pregnant ladies be fat? And glowing? Is that why the doctor told you to take it easy?'

'Why would you do this? Ruin your career?' She hadn't read it all but she had read enough.

'I'm not ruining my career. I'm proposing to you.' He dragged the chair by the dressing table over to the window so that he was sitting next to her.

'Why did you let them print all that stuff?' Francesca whispered. 'Now the whole world knows about…our involvement…and my background…' Her eyes flickered down, seeking out the details of her past once again and re-reading them. In stark black and white it sounded even grimmer because there was no attempt to portray extenuating circumstances.

'It was the only way.' He shook his head and did something that was unbearably touching. He played nervously with her fingers. Francesca watched his down-bent head as the questions raced through her mind. In the most public way possible, Angelo Falcone had proposed to her, taking the bull by the horns and giving the media what they would eventually discover anyway, namely her past. But why? Did it mean that much to him that his baby was born with the Falcone name? Because there was no mention of love.

He raised his eyes to her. 'When I left you a week ago, I didn't know what to think. Not only was there the fatherhood situation to deal with, but in the space of an hour you had managed to trample everything I thought I knew about you into the ground.' It was only when she had revealed everything to him that Angelo had realised, with a sickening sense of utter shock, exactly how much he had drifted into a comfort zone. Despite all his declarations of non-involvement, he had grown used to her. Like ivy curling around a column she had entwined herself around him and the pieces of her past, the past that made the present, dammit, had been like the bitter stab of treachery.

'I'm sorry. I should have told you sooner, years before, but I knew that things would end the minute you found out about me. You're not an ordinary man, Angelo. If you were, it wouldn't have been so bad.' She risked stroking his hair and he pulled her hand to him and held it. 'Ordinary men aren't in the public gaze. They can handle a woman with a dodgy background.'

'I've been to hell and back this week, Francesca, but the one thing I know is that I want this baby of ours to have a family.'

'And if I weren't pregnant, Angelo? Would you still have taken out an ad in the newspaper letting the world know that you wanted to marry me or would you have counted yourself lucky to have got away?'

'If you read the article carefully, my darling, you would see that at no point did I mention the fact that you are pregnant. Everything else, yes, but that, no.'

So he hadn't mentioned anything about being in love with her, but nevertheless a little tendril of hope began to uncurl inside of her.

'Because...?'

'Because I want you for my wife, Francesca, whether you happen to be carrying my child or not.' He looked at her steadily, willing himself to say what he needed to say in a way that wouldn't frighten her off. 'When we embarked on this crazy...affair, we both knew the rules. Sex without commitment. We would finish what had been started years ago and emotion wouldn't get in the way.'

Why was he reminding her of things she didn't want to remember? After he had called her *my darling* and looked at her with eyes that promised even if they hadn't delivered?

'But emotion did get in the way, after all. At least, it got in my way.'

'I beg your pardon?' She leaned towards him, straining to hear every single word he was saying.

'I thought I was in control, but it turns out I wasn't.' He shot her a rueful smile. 'And, before you say anything, just hear me out and then decide what you want to do. Whatever you want, Francesca, I'll fall in line with.' He breathed in deeply and expelled his breath in one long sigh. 'I know you didn't choose to become pregnant. I was so wrapped up in my own thoughts and then so gutted by what you told me that it never even crossed my mind to ask how you felt about having a baby and for that I'm...I'm sorry. This...is difficult for me...'

He stood up and paced the room, his movements agitated. Francesca had never seen him like this before, and she reckoned she had probably seen him in all his moods. It was a revelation of vulnerability. Finally he returned to the chair and sat down, resting his elbows on his knees. 'I've spent the week going over in my head everything that's happened between us. You made a big deal of letting me know that you were willing to let me walk away from you, or rather you walk away from me, because you didn't feel that your background would do me any favours. It occurred to me that maybe I had got it all wrong from the start. Maybe you just didn't want to be hooked up with me. Maybe behind the smokescreen was someone who just wasn't willing to spend her life with someone who had all the privileges of wealth. It struck me that you might be physically attracted to a man like me but emotionally attracted to a man like Jack when it came to a permanent relationship.' He took a deep breath and shook his head. Was he even making sense? He knew exactly what he wanted to say but he could feel that the words were not emerging from his mouth in quite the order he would have liked. For the first time, his formidable grasp of the English language had deserted him. 'Women are attracted to me. They like the wealth, the power, the status.' He gave a dry laugh. 'Georgina being a case in point. Fact is, though, you're not like other women and so all the usual yardsticks no longer apply. Do you understand what I'm trying to say?'

Francesca nodded slowly. 'I think so…'

'I'm glad you're pregnant, Francesca. I'm over the moon that you're having my baby but I meant what I said. I want to marry you, baby or not, because I…because I realise that sleeping with you wasn't enough for me.' He gave her a crooked smile but underneath she could see that he was drained. 'Call me a greedy man, but I want more than just your beautiful body. I want your mind, your heart, your soul, because you have mine. All those things. They're yours. They belonged to you three years ago when you walked out on me and they belong to you now. If you'll have them. I hope you do and I hope that you'll marry me even if I have to spend the rest of my days winning your love. Even if, right now, you may not think me the right man for you.' Over the past torturous week Angelo had figured out what it was about love that set it aside from everything he had ever experienced in his life before. Aside from being the one thing over which he exerted no control, it was also a humbling experience. He was hanging on for dear life to what she would say.

'That's a tall order, Angelo.'

He paled. In one short sentence, his world came crashing down.

'I mean,' Francesca continued thoughtfully, 'it takes a lot to win my love.'

'I'll do anything.'

'Romantic gestures?' She frowned. 'You know, flowers et cetera, little love notes dotted around…'

Angelo looked at the slow smile tugging at the corners of her mouth. 'Yes, I can do flowers et cetera.'

'Candlelit dinners now and again—cooked by you, of course…'

He raised his eyebrows and looked doubtful. 'You drive a hard bargain but I'm willing to give it a go.'

'Breakfast in bed every morning?'

'Seriously pushing your luck here.'

'Then how about sex on demand?'

'I think I can manage that.'

'I love you, Angelo.' She looked at him with shining eyes. 'I fell in love with you years ago and that's why I never told you the truth about myself, my background. I thought that you would drop me like a hot potato the minute you found out and, the longer I left it, the more of a mountain it became until there was no way out but to leave, but I've been hurting all this time.' She leaned towards him and kissed him, melting into his arms, letting him carry her over to the bed—but no sex, he told her, not until her doctor had given her the go-ahead.

So they talked. Once he started, Angelo found that the words poured out of him, words that had never crossed his lips before. He could remember Georgina asking him if he loved her, could remember his reply that love was an illusion, something people clung on to because it made them feel safer, less isolated. It had seemed a perfectly reasonable response to him at the time. No longer.

Francesca, caught up in the rapture of the unbelievable, could have listened to him for ever. She quizzed him over and over about whether he was certain that he could marry a woman with a colourful past and was ridiculously pleased when he told her that her past was a damn sight more interesting than anyone else's he could think of. What she saw as a liability he viewed as an asset, and Francesca didn't know whether to believe him or not, but what she did know was that he would protect her from anyone who might ever dare to question his decision. The rush of love that filled her made her tremble.

'Do you realise,' Angelo said, eventually drawing her to him, 'I've never had as many unofficial days off work with any woman as I've had with you? And yet we've never been on holiday together. We'll just have to put that right while there are just the two of us to consider...'

They did. Three months later, for their honeymoon on a tiny island in the Caribbean. The wedding had been small—just a few close friends and family and no paparazzi. Francesca had no idea how he had managed to pull that off but, as he'd wryly told her, today's gossip became yesterday's fish and chips' wrapping in the blink of an eye.

With her pregnancy now beginning to show, Francesca wore a range of loose clothing and one-piece swimsuits, ignoring Angelo's urges that she show her swelling stomach proudly. Everything about her pregnancy made him proud.

Through the open windows of their little wooden cabana she could hear the sound of the sea lapping against the shore and outside was inky black.

Angelo was standing in front of the mirror, absent-mindedly trying to tidy his hair without the use of a comb, towel slung low on his hips because he had just emerged from the shower.

He caught her eye in the mirror and grinned. 'Are you doing that on purpose?' he asked, turning around. 'Lying there with that sexy little smile on your face? You know what it's going to do to me...' As if to prove his point, he released the towel and revealed his arousal.

'You mean I still turn you on even though I no longer possess that model figure that used to drive you crazy?' As if she needed reassuring. He had proved to her over and over again just how much she still turned him on. He delighted in her blossoming figure and adored the heavy fullness of her breasts and the darkening of her nipples, which had become much larger and more pronounced.

Now he knelt by the side of the bed and, as she rolled over to face him, he lazily lifted her lacy pyjama top to reveal the exquisite bounty of her breasts, which lay like ripened fruit waiting for his attention.

Francesca watched with loving eyes as he delicately traced the full, dark circle, then the hardened tip, with his tongue before drawing the nipple into his mouth and suckling on it. With one hand he caressed her stomach and she groaned softly, parting her legs to invite his hand there.

This was her man and this was the very, very wonderful life she had never imagined she could ever have.

SPECIAL EDITION

Life, Love and Family

These contemporary romances will strike a chord with you as heroines juggle life and relationships on their way to true love.

New York Times bestselling author Linda Lael Miller brings you a BRAND-NEW contemporary story featuring her fan-favorite McKettrick family.

Meg McKettrick is surprised to be reunited with her high school flame, Brad O''Ballivan. After enjoying a career as a country-and-western singer, Brad aches for a home and family...and seeing Meg again makes him realize he still loves her. But their pride manages to interfere with love... until an unexpected matchmaker gets involved.

Turn the page for a sneak preview of
THE MCKETTRICK WAY by Linda Lael Miller
On sale November 20, wherever books are sold.

Brad shoved the truck into gear and drove to the bottom of the hill, where the road forked. Turn left, and he'd be home in five minutes. Turn right, and he was headed for Indian Rock.

He had no damn business going to Indian Rock.

He had nothing to say to Meg McKettrick, and if he never set eyes on the woman again, it would be two weeks too soon.

He turned right.

He couldn't have said why.

He just drove straight to the Dixie Dog Drive-In.

Back in the day, he and Meg used to meet at the Dixie Dog, by tacit agreement, when either of them had been away. It had been some kind of universe thing, purely intuitive.

Passing familiar landmarks, Brad told himself he ought to turn around. The old days were gone. Things had ended badly between him and Meg anyhow, and she wasn't going to be at the Dixie Dog.

He kept driving.

He rounded a bend, and there was the Dixie Dog. Its big neon sign, a giant hot dog, was all lit up and going through its corny sequence..first it was covered in red squiggles of light, meant to suggest ketchup, and then yellow, for mustard.

Brad pulled into one of the slots next to a speaker, rolled down the truck window and ordered.

A girl roller-skated out with the order about five minutes later.

When she wheeled up to the driver's window, smiling, her eyes went wide with recognition, and she dropped the tray with a clatter.

Silently Brad swore. Damn if he hadn't forgotten he was a famous country singer.

The girl, a skinny thing wearing too much eye makeup, immediately started to cry. ''I'm sorry!'' she sobbed, squatting to gather up the mess.

''It's okay,'' Brad answered quietly, leaning to look down at her, catching a glimpse of her plastic name tag. ''It's okay, Mandy. No harm done.''

''I'll get you another dog and a shake right away, Mr. O'Ballivan!''

''Mandy?''

She stared up at him pitifully, sniffling. Thanks to the copious tears, most of the goop on her eyes had slid south. ''Yes?''

''When you go back inside, could you not mention seeing me?''

''But you're Brad O'Ballivan!''

''Yeah,'' he answered, suppressing a sigh. ''I know.''

She rolled a little closer. ''You wouldn't happen to have a picture you could autograph for me, would you?''

''Not with me,'' Brad answered.

''You could sign this napkin, though,'' Mandy said. ''It's only got a little chocolate on the corner.''

Brad took the paper napkin and her order pen, and scrawled his name. Handed both items back through the window.

She turned and whizzed back toward the side entrance to the Dixie Dog.

Brad waited, marveling that he hadn't considered incidents like this one before he'd decided to come back home.

In retrospect, it seemed shortsighted, to say the least, but the truth was, he'd expected to be.. Brad O'Ballivan.

Presently Mandy skated back out again, and this time she managed to hold on to the tray.

"I didn't tell a soul!" she whispered. "But Heather and Darlene both asked me why my mascara was all smeared." Efficiently she hooked the tray onto the bottom edge of the window.

Brad extended payment, but Mandy shook her head.

"The boss said it's on the house, since I dumped your first order on the ground."

He smiled. "Okay, then. Thanks."

Mandy retreated, and Brad was just reaching for the food when a bright red Blazer whipped into the space beside his. The driver's door sprang open, crashing into the metal speaker, and somebody got out in a hurry.

Something quickened inside Brad.

And in the next moment Meg McKettrick was standing practically on his running board, her blue eyes blazing.

Brad grinned. "I guess you're not over me after all," he said.

HARLEQUIN *Presents*

THE ROYAL HOUSE OF NIROLI

Always passionate, always proud.

**The richest royal family in the world—
a family united by blood and passion,
torn apart by deceit and desire.**

By royal decree, Harlequin Presents is delighted to bring you
The Royal House of Niroli. Step into the glamorous, enticing
world of the Nirolian Royal Family. As the king ails he
must find an heir…each month an exciting new installment
follows the epic search for the true Nirolian king. Eight heirs,
eight passionate romances, eight fantastic stories!

Coming in December:

THE PRINCE'S FORBIDDEN VIRGIN
by Robyn Donald
Book #2683

**Although Rosa Fierezza knows he's forbidden fruit,
she's under Max's spell. However, just when Rosa and
Max give up all hope of being together, the truth about
a scandal from the past may set them free….**

*Be sure not to miss the next book
in this fabulous series!*

Coming in January:
BRIDE BY ROYAL APPOINTMENT
by Raye Morgan Book #2691

HARLEQUIN *Presents*

IN Bed WITH THE BOSS

Chosen by him for business,
taken by him for pleasure…

A classic collection of office romances from
Harlequin Presents by your favorite authors

ITALIAN BOSS,
HOUSEKEEPER BRIDE
by Sharon Kendrick
Book #2687

Raffael needs a fiancée—and he's chosen his mousy
housekeeper Natasha! They have to pretend to be
engaged, but neither has to fake the explosive
attraction between them….

Available December 2007 wherever you buy books.

Look out for more sexy bosses,
coming soon in Harlequin Presents!

REQUEST YOUR FREE BOOKS!

HARLEQUIN® Presents®

2 FREE NOVELS
PLUS 2
FREE GIFTS!

PASSION GUARANTEED SEDUCTION

HP07